NINE LIVES

IN DOG TOWN

SANDY RIDEOUT

ELLEN RIGGS

FREE PREQUEL

A Rescue Dog and an Unexpected Date with Destiny

Meet Isla McInnis, a reporter who flies across the country to Dorset Hills on a hunch that a sweet little rescue dog named Rio will change her life forever. A quirky band of rescue rebels shows her the true reason she was called to this quaint town in the first place. Join Sandy Rideout's author newsletter at **Sandyrideout.com** to get the FREE PREQUEL to the Dog Town cozy-romance series at sandyrideout.com.

Nine Lives in Dog Town

Copyright © 2019 Sandy Rideout

ISBN 978-1-989303-31-3 eBook
ISBN 978-1-989303-87-0 Book
ASIN B07NKJS2KS Kindle
ASIN TBD Paperback

Publisher: Sandy Rideout
www.sandyrideout.com
Cover designer: Lou Harper
Editor: Serena Clarke
2111050654

CONTENTS

WELCOME TO DOG TOWN!

Dear Reader,

I used to be a diehard cat lady. Then I got my first dog ever and I was a goner! A journalist by training, I interviewed every expert I could find: trainers, breeders, groomers, walkers and more. The journey ultimately brought me here, to Dog Town.

Dorset Hills, better known as *Dog Town*, is famous for being the most dog-friendly place in the world. People come from near and far to enjoy its beautiful landscape and unique charms. Naturally, when so many dogs and dog-lovers unite in one town, mischief and mayhem ensue.

In the Dog Town cozy-romance series, you can expect the humor, the quirky, loveable characters and the edge-of-your-seat suspense that are part of any cozy mystery, but there's a little more romance and a lot less murder. In fact, *no one dies!* I can guarantee you'll laugh out loud and enjoy hair-raising adventures, heartwarming holidays and happily-ever-afters for both humans and pets.

You can read the books in any order, but it's more fun to work your way through the seasons in Dog Town:

- *Ready or Not in Dog Town* (The Beginning)
- *Bitter and Sweet in Dog Town* (Labor Day)
- *A Match Made in Dog Town* (Thanksgiving)

- *Lost and Found in Dog Town* (Christmas)
- *Calm and Bright in Dog Town* (Christmas)
- *Tried and True in Dog Town* (New Year's)
- *Yours and Mine in Dog Town* (Valentine's Day)
- *Nine Lives in Dog Town* (Easter)
- *Great and Small in Dog Town* (Memorial Day)
- *Bold and Blue in Dog Town* (Independence Day)
- *Better or Worse in Dog Town* (Labor Day)

If you fancy more murder with your mystery, be sure to join my newsletter at **Sandyrideout.com** to get the FREE PREQUEL to the Bought-the-Farm Cozy Mystery series. My newsletter is filled with funny stories and photos of my adorable dogs. Don't miss out!

Take care,
Sandy (and Ellen)

CHAPTER ONE

Evie Springdale had done her homework on Dorset Hills. She'd read the articles, studied social media and watched every video clip she could find. But nothing had quite prepared her for the massive German shepherd sitting in the middle of Bellington Square outside City Hall. The dog was eight feet tall, with feral-looking eyes, teeth like scythes and pricked ears large enough to detect signals from outer space. The beast was the perfect image of the wolf in Little Red Riding Hood, and since Evie's childhood nickname was "Red," that seemed like an ominous sign.

"Isn't she remarkable?" Mayor Bradshaw asked. "Eight hundred pounds of brass."

"Remarkable, yes," Evie said, clearing her throat. "Striking."

"I will say she's the least popular among the collection, and yet the most realistic."

She circled the dog. "Perhaps that's the problem, sir. I noticed on the website kids were crying in the shots with this statue."

The mayor's silver eyebrows lifted and then settled.

"Coincidence, I'm sure. But I'll have someone remove those photos." He made a sweeping gesture that took in the sparkling gold brick of the City Hall building and its clock tower. "Dorset Hills is a magnet for dog-lovers. People come clear across the country to see this, you know."

"I do know," Evie said. "I did."

She'd flown in from San Francisco two weeks earlier to visit her brother, Nick, and was intrigued enough by Dog Town to stay for a while. Nick had pulled a few strings to get her a meeting with the mayor.

"And what's the verdict?" he asked.

"It's everything I imagined. And so much more."

Mayor Bradshaw nodded. "This was just your average hillside town 10 years ago. One article naming us the best place in North America for dogs and dog-lovers changed all that. Now we can't keep people away."

"Such a unique claim to fame," Evie said, following him over the cobblestones as they left Bellington Square and turned onto Main Street. She wished she hadn't worn heels, but it wouldn't have felt right to meet the mayor in flats. Luckily his progress was slow because people kept stopping him to say hello. He pressed more palms in a short block than a movie star.

"Here's our St. Bernard," he said, stopping in front of the hospital.

The bronze beast was less imposing than the German shepherd, but she shuddered at the thought of the slobber and fur that would come with a dog that size.

"Charming," she said.

She hadn't expected the mayor to introduce her personally to notable landmarks. As a political public relations consultant for nearly 10 years, she figured she'd seen it all, but Dorset Hills surprised her. The bronze statues, the dog-themed diners and businesses and the vast number of actual dogs made it seem like a cartoon. Not that she'd ever say so. Her brother had warned her that City Council took its branding very seriously.

"Do they talk about us?" the mayor asked. "In San Francisco?"

"Oh, yes. I'd heard about Dog Town long before my brother decided to move here."

That was true and also the reason she'd thought Nick had lost his mind. He'd fallen hard for a pretty dog trainer, however, and would have followed her to the ends of the earth. That Evie understood; she'd done silly things for love, too. What stunned her was that he'd stayed after the trainer was history, and built a successful technology business. He said he'd put down roots for Clive, his golden retriever, but there had to be more to it than that. Maybe now that they lived a few blocks apart she could figure out what made her brother tick.

The mayor posed for a selfie with a woman and her cherubic toddler. Then he turned back to Evie and said, "Your brother tells me you're a spin doctor and a fixer."

She made a mental note to give her brother more appropriate key messages. "I've worked in public relations for 10 years."

"I guess a fixer never admits to that, does she?" He ushered her through an archway and into the courtyard of the Barton Gallery of Art. The noise from Main Street receded, drowned by the sound of rushing water from a large fountain. To their left was an outdoor café that bustled despite the chilly breeze. It was spring, but even the seasons operated at a slower pace in Dorset Hills.

"Do you need public relations support, sir?" she asked, following him to the entrance of the gallery. A small gasp escaped her at the sight of two gigantic wolfhounds flanking the double oak doors. "Oh my."

He chuckled at her reaction. "These were our first. A gift from the billionaire Pemberton family."

Evie stared up at the twin dogs and swallowed hard. "I don't know what to say."

"Nick said you *always* know what to say. That's why I'm interested in hiring you."

She tore her eyes from the terrifying dogs and looked up at him. He reminded her of an aging movie star her mom had liked, someone who played hero or villain with equal panache.

"I admire what you've accomplished with the Dog Town branding," she said. "In fact, I've never seen anything like it."

"You will. It'll sink its teeth into you."

She laughed. "Maybe. It worked on my brother, and we weren't raised with pets."

"I feel sorry for you." He leaned over to scratch a bronze dog's chest, as if it were real. "Dogs are the greatest comfort in the world."

"I thought you gave up your poodle, sir. I heard about Princess through the grapevine."

He shot her a dark glance. "Well, you don't know everything, I'm sure of that." He walked over to the fountain and stared into the water before turning to sit down. "Losing Princess hit me hard—so hard that I had to do some soul-searching." He patted the space beside him in an invitation. "Thankfully, that inner work is yielding rewards."

Evie eyed the damp stone and stayed where she was. Her linen skirt wouldn't fare well on that, nor would her curly hair in the mist from the fountain.

"I'm sure it's been stressful here lately, what with the bad press over dog court," she said.

The City's crackdown on canine delinquents had backfired terribly. The first judge left in January after just a few weeks in the role. In February, the next judge made some bad calls and court was disbanded. Now, in late March, as the sun called out the flowers, the mayor seemed chastened.

"It's only temporary," he said. "We can't have dogs running amok, but dog court didn't go as planned." He stared around the courtyard. "Sometimes I wonder if I get the best advice."

"Sir?"

His lips pressed in a thin line. "It takes courage to speak truth to power. Can you do that?"

"Of course. You don't survive long in politics if you can't speak hard truths."

"Then tell me about getting fired, Evelyn."

She'd known the question was coming because it always did. "Someone disagreed with how I handled an issue and showed me the door. It comes with the territory, unfortunately. I'm happy to find new opportunities and love the idea of working in a small town."

"Not that small." He patted the stone again and she pretended not to notice. "So, if I dropped into your house, what would be the biggest surprise waiting for me?"

It was an odd question but she tried to go with the flow. "My extensive cat collection, I suppose."

"Cats! I'm not a fan. They kill our beautiful birds and they're impossible to control. We're introducing new regulations to keep them in check." He caught himself. "That's in confidence, please. Every new policy seems to raise hackles. I've hired a new chief of staff to handle these things for me."

"Well, my cat collection is above the law because it's art.

My mom wouldn't let us have pets, so she gives me cat-themed gifts. Glass, pewter, wood, you name it. I do try to contain it in one room."

"Like Bluebeard's chamber?"

"Exactly." She waited a beat and asked, "What would surprise me in *your* house, sir? Metaphorically speaking?"

"All politicians have a thing or two to hide, no? It's how people like you stay in business."

It sounded dirty when he said it. It often felt dirty when she did it. Back in journalism school, she'd dreamed of being a mystery novelist. Instead she had gone from one risky PR job to another, leaving a trail of crumpled resumes behind her.

"I thought it might be different here. Dorset Hills is so pretty and friendly."

Crossing his legs, he exposed gray socks with tiny black poodles on them. "The first commandment of Dorset Hills is *Thou must love dogs*." He fixed her with a level stare. "Do you?"

"My doggie nephew Clive has opened a new world to me. He's a sweet charmer."

"Golden retrievers always are. But you didn't answer my question."

"Mayor Bradshaw... Who doesn't love dogs?"

"Another evasion." His eyes sharpened. "You're worse than me, Evelyn. Dogs are our brand. Our reason for being. Only a dog-lover could understand what we're about here. Cat-lovers need not apply."

Finally, she perched on the dank stone, smoothing her skirt as she did. "I said I'd be honest, so here it is: I'm nervous around animals and I have terrible allergies. But I fully understand what Dorset Hills is about and I don't have to own a dog to advocate for all you do here."

"You need to understand us. To be one of us."

He pulled out his phone and she knew she was losing him. Losing the opportunity. That bothered her more than she expected. Another job always came along and she'd promised herself to get out of politics anyway. Better to work in that pretty little café than get dragged through the mud again. And yet.... And yet... She wanted this job. Dorset Hills was stunningly beautiful, with rolling green hills on one side and a sapphire lake on the other. It was surprisingly cultured for a city of this size, with art galleries, a museum and lovely gardens and parks. More importantly, it was a place to write her story anew. In a year, she'd be established in the community and could move into something else. Political life wasn't her true calling—eight firings had proven that—but until she knew for sure what she was put on the planet to do, it would have to suffice. Whatever her shortcomings, she had the experience to steer this quirky town out of troubled waters.

"You know what you need, Mayor? Distraction. People are still talking about dog court because you haven't given them a new story. A good news story. What is Dorset Hills doing to help dogs? You need a mission tied in with your brand that everyone can get behind."

He looked up from his phone. "And that is...?"

"I have ideas. In the short term, all you need is a fun event for Easter."

"We always have our parade."

"Shake it up. How about an Easter festival instead? A treasure hunt for both children and dogs."

He looked at his phone again. "What else have you got?"

A movement caught her eye. The toddler who'd been in the selfie earlier was racing after a small dog. The dog leapt onto the rim of the fountain beside the mayor and the child clambered after it. There was a splash as dog and child tumbled into the fountain. Evie lifted her legs and spun around. The water wasn't deep, but the little boy was thrashing and gasping. Standing up in the fountain, she grabbed the child and quickly passed him to his mother when she ran over. Her shrieks turned to sobs and she hugged him, shaking.

"He's fine," Evie said, climbing out of the fountain. "Everything's fine. Look, he's not even crying."

"You saved him," the woman said, grabbing Evie's arm. "Thank you so much."

"Credit goes to the mayor, actually," Evie said. "He saw it first."

Mayor Bradshaw raised both hands. "It was nothing, really. I'm just glad your boy is okay."

"May I take a photo?" Evie asked. "Such a happy moment!"

The little boy buried his face in his mother's shoulder, but the woman managed a tremulous smile as Evie snapped the photo.

As they exchanged names and said their goodbyes, Evie leaned over and collected her purse from the water. She followed the mayor out of the square, squelching with every step. Her pink suede pumps were toast, not to mention everything in her purse.

"Nicely done, Evelyn," he said, as they took the back alleys to City Hall.

When they got to Bellington Square, two men in city coveralls were leaning over a garden with some sort of power tool.

"Are those blow dryers?" she asked.

"Indeed. Heat opens the tulips. They're late this year

and I want things perfect for my meeting with Hannah Pemberton tomorrow. She's interested in investing in Dorset Hills." He stopped at the bottom of the stairs and eyed her damp outfit. "No need to come in. You can pitch your Easter festival to the team tomorrow."

"Does that mean I'm hired?"

"I suppose it's the least I can do after your heroics."

"Actually, sir, you can pick up the tab for my shoes. The story of you saving the child will hit the news."

"If it does, I'll cover the purse, too," he said, starting up the stairs.

"I'll need a new phone to do my job," she called.

He came back down. "You're pushy. I don't like that."

"Everyone likes pushy when it's on their team."

"Don't make me fire you again, Evelyn."

The deal was sealed with a disappointingly limp handshake. Regardless, there was a spring in her step as she left Bellington Square. Her ninth life had begun.

CHAPTER TWO

It was dusk by the time she pulled up in front of the rundown two-story house she'd rented on impulse. She'd only planned to visit her brother for a week or two, but when this place came up, it felt like a sign. It didn't make sense, since she wasn't a dog lover, but the quirky city seemed ideal for overcoming career calamity out in the real world. Her brother had encouraged her to stay with him, but she wanted her own space. Nick and Clive had their routine.

The market was so tight in Dorset Hills that she felt lucky to have found a place just blocks from her brother's house in the Riverdale neighborhood. The landlord had apparently given up on it, so she'd need to hire a handyman to spruce it up a little. It would suit her needs for now, and with her history of moving around there was no point in a big commitment.

Just as she touched the rusty screen door, there was a muffled squawk. Jumping back, she peered through the mesh. Crouching between the doors was a fluffy animal that looked about the size of a raccoon. The second squawk sounded more like a strangled mew, however.

Evie groped for her phone in her pocket and turned on the flashlight before gingerly pulling open the screen door. A marmalade tabby cat emerged slowly. His next mew was stronger and he almost seemed to swagger as he came toward her.

"Hey, little buddy," she said. "How did you get stuck between the doors?"

Now came a drawn-out meow, with a plaintive twang that suggested he'd been there a while.

Bending, she stroked his head and shoulders, and then felt for a collar but found none. Her hand came away wet, and when she turned the light, she saw blood on her fingertips.

"Oh no, you poor thing. You're hurt."

She managed to get her keys out of her bag with her left hand and unlocked the door without getting blood on anything. The cat didn't wait for an invitation. He slipped past her and walked into the house. Elbowing the light switch, she headed into the kitchen to wash the blood off her hand.

When she turned, her guest was standing on the black and white kitchen tiles staring up at her with wide green eyes. He was a large cat, but so thin that his fur seemed a size too big. One ear was ragged and his coat was dull, either from poor nutrition or neglecting his grooming.

"You're a mess, my friend. What am I going to do with you?" She sneezed twice in quick succession. "I'm afraid you can't stay long, because I'm allergic to you."

Undeterred, he walked over and swished a figure eight between her feet. His mew took on a pleading tone and it sounded like he was trying to purr. He must be famished.

The cupboards were pretty bare, as she'd never gotten into the habit of cooking and most of her things were still in boxes. Luckily there were a couple of tins of tuna. She took the can opener out of the drawer and sneezed again as the cat circled her legs, his purr-meow escalating in volume. Prying off the lid, she dumped the whole tin into a bowl, crushed the fish with a fork, and then set the bowl on the floor. "Bon appetit."

He dug in with none of a cat's usual delicacy and in less than a minute the bowl was empty. Looping through her legs again, he asked for more.

"Business first. Stay here." She went into the bathroom and came back with a large towel. Draping it over the round oak pedestal table, she turned on another light. "Do you mind if I pick you up?"

A college roommate had owned cats, and she knew felines often preferred to keep four on the floor. They'd kick and struggle, leaving scratches that turned to angry hives. But Mr. Marmalade seemed friendly enough—possibly because he was hoping for more tuna.

When she bent to lift him, he pushed off with his back paws, as if to help launch. He was lighter than she expected, and as skinny as she'd feared. Setting him gently on the kitchen table, she aimed her phone flashlight at his shoulder and gently brushed back the fur. The cat flinched but held his ground. Leaning in, she saw what appeared to be two puncture marks in the middle of an angry red swelling. The wound oozed blood, and from the smell of it, also pus.

"Oh my, something got you good." Another volley of four-five-six sneezes sent her reeling to the roll of paper towels on the counter. Her eyes prickled and she knew they'd be puffing up. "We're going to need to call for reinforcements, buddy," she said, wiping her nose. "Hang tight."

The cat curled up on the towel, tail over his nose, and closed his eyes.

"I'M NOT your knight in shining armor, Evie."

Nick leaned against her kitchen counter and crossed his arms. His expression was a mixture of bemusement and disgust. He had no affinity for cats but she knew he wouldn't be unkind to one, either.

"That's for sure." She sniffled as she eyed him up and down. Her brother hadn't bothered to change out of his old sweats with holes in the knees before responding to her text. His hair, a deeper, richer red than hers, was sticking out all over, and he had two days' growth of stubble. "My knight in shining armor would never leave the house looking like that."

"Your knight in shining armor got knocked off his steed and died. Eight times, as I recall."

She sighed. "Eight wrongs don't make a knight."

He gave his trademark barky laugh and she laughed, too. Her brother teased her mercilessly, but he meant well. That's why she'd come to Dog Town after her latest debacle instead of running home to her parents. As much as Nick teased, he really didn't judge, unlike their mom. He wanted the best for her, she was sure of that, but he wasn't a pushover either.

"If you want to help this guy, take him to the vet," he said. "I'm not getting stuck with a stray cat. I've got enough on my plate with Clive."

His dog had been a handful and she knew he was counting on what experts said to be true: that retrievers matured into placid dogs at age three. There was only one more year to go.

"I can't do it." She sneezed into her sleeve. "Just look at me."

"You're a mess," he agreed. "Too bad you got the freckles and the orange hair." He looked at the cat. "Hey, you guys match."

"Too bad you got the bad attitude and the beady eyes," she said. Her green eyes were her best feature, whereas Nick's were a swampy hazel. Still, there was no mistaking they were siblings. "And too bad I got the allergies. That's why I'm renting this dump instead of living free with you and your fur machine."

He rolled his muddy eyes. "Never have I seen someone go through an entire lint roller in a day. I don't know how you're going to survive an orange cat."

"I'm not, that's how. I just want to get him fixed up. You can leave him with the vet and I'm sure they'll place him. I'll pay the bills, of course."

"I'm not going to dump-and-run for you. Do your own dirty work." He smirked. "Isn't that your job?"

"Very funny." Nick had never had much respect for her work. In fact, political machinations made him cringe. That had left them with little to talk about, because her life revolved around work. Actually, they'd never had much in common. He'd been popular in high school, somehow straddling the line between being a star athlete and a nerdy video game addict, whereas she'd been a studious wallflower. "If you have such contempt for my vocation, why did you hook me up with the mayor?"

He shrugged. "The way things have been going I thought it would be good for the town to have someone with a kind heart advising Council."

"Thank you. But will he listen? He said he wanted someone to 'speak truth to power,' but most politicians only think so if you agree with them."

Nick pushed off the counter and circled the kitchen table. The cat slit open his eyes and watched him. As she suspected, he'd only been pretending to sleep through the discussion.

"You'll need to watch your back with Bill Bradshaw," Nick said.

"I can handle myself. He won't be the sleaziest leader I've worked for."

Picking up a spatula from the dish rack, Nick gave her a swat on the arm. "Maybe not, but an older brother worries."

She grabbed the spatula and swatted him back. "Those nine minutes you've got on me haven't made you worldly. I've seen things that would curl your hair. If it weren't already curly."

Grabbing a soup ladle, he made another jab, but she feinted. "Is that why you're hiding out in the land of dogs?"

"Pretty much, yeah. I need a breath of fresh air."

Nick gestured to the cat, who was decidedly stinky. "That's fresh?"

"As fresh as your dog. He smells fishy all the time."

"That's what retrievers smell like." His brows came together in a rare frown. She'd hit a nerve, and she'd have to remember exactly where it was so she could poke it again at her convenience.

"Anyway," he said, changing the subject. "The mayor just brought on Zeke Mackey as chief of staff. Zeke and I play hockey together and he's a stand-up guy. I expect you two to turn things around."

"So, no pressure then? Just put the heart back in the town and turn it around?"

"That's all," he said, leaning over the cat. "And don't get your ass fired again. Eight times in 10 years has got to be some kind of record."

She knew he was joking but flinched anyway. "It's politics. Besides, you got fired a couple of times. That's why you had to start your own company."

The cat leaned away from Nick, tail twitching. It was obvious he didn't like being crowded but Nick wasn't always sensitive.

"No one can fire me now," he agreed. "Except clients. And the City's a big contract for me, so make me look good, okay?"

She started walking toward them and stepped on the china bowl that had held the tuna. It crushed under her foot and she turned her ankle on the pieces.

Nick reached out a hand to steady her. "As graceful as ever, I see. It's like your parts don't all work together."

"Tell me about it." She'd had several accidents over the years, and had the lumps and scars to prove it. Their mom had always said she had her head in the clouds instead of on what she was doing.

Nick turned and crossed to the front door in a couple of easy strides. "Be right back."

"Don't worry," she told the cat, gently stroking his chin. There were hives on the back of her hand from where he'd licked her earlier. "Nick will take care of you, I'm sure of it."

In less than a minute he came back in with a plastic pet carrier. "Put him in this so he doesn't crap in your car."

"Nick! You can't just leave me to deal with a cat."

"You and stink bomb will be just fine," he said.

"Roberto," she said.

"Roberto? You've named him?" He sounded incredulous.

"I didn't name him. That's just his name."

It sounded odd, but it also felt true. Even if she felt like naming a cat, which she didn't, it would never be something affected like "Roberto."

Her brother walked back to the door and turned. "You never used to be this weird," he said.

"Politics will do that to a person." She glared after him. "Thanks for nothing, big brother."

CHAPTER THREE

A blinding light hit Evie directly in the eyes and her hand flew up to shield them. "Ow!"

"Sorry, sorry." The veterinarian covered the head lamp with his gloved hand. He was wearing safety goggles as well. "I just wanted to tell you that the tissues are on the counter."

Her eyes and nose were still streaming and her sniffing must have been driving him nuts as he examined the cat. Nick said Dr. Benson was the best vet in town. Technically, his office was on the outskirts, which meant his prices were a little lower.

Reaching for the box of flimsy tissues, she grabbed a handful. "How does he look?"

"Not as bad as I feared." He leaned over the cat again. "There's nothing to get so upset about, really."

Did he think she was crying? "I'm not upset. I just have terrible allergies. This guy couldn't have picked a worse place to get stuck in a door."

"He could, actually. Not everyone in Dorset Hills

would be so kind to a stray cat. Felines have fallen out of favor recently."

Evie chafed at her nose, knowing it was already bright red. "I've always kind of admired cats—from a safe distance." She looked up at images flashing across a video monitor, presumably of his patients. There were gerbils, birds, rabbits, guinea pigs and even a hedgehog. "I see you've got a broad clientele."

"I'm the only vet in town specializing in small animals and aviary medicine," he said. "If you've got a sick rat, I'm your man."

He glanced up again, steering the headlamp with caution. His eyes were bright blue behind the goggles and his teeth were white and even. It surprised her that she even noticed he was geekily handsome. She was only six weeks out of her last breakup, and it usually took longer than that to appreciate men again. In fact, she'd sworn off them during her time in Dog Town. She likely wouldn't last here, so what was the point? Besides, she'd had eight relationships in the past 10 years—some more serious than others—and most had ended badly. She'd wasn't about to blow her ninth romantic life on just anyone.

"Good to know," she said. "Although I'm 110 per cent sure I'll never have cause for a rat specialist."

"Don't rule it out. They're surprisingly great pets. Very social."

"Dr. Benson?"

"Call me Jon."

"Okay, then... Jon? There is no way in a million years I'll invite a rodent into my life. They're totally creepy. I'd rather have my eyes picked out by eagles than—"

"I get the picture," he said, laughing. "I could help with the eagles, too, actually."

Now she laughed. "You're a modern Dr. Doolittle. A man of many species."

"These days it's just dog after dog after dog," he said. "Obviously I've got nothing against dogs." He waved a medical instrument toward the large black and tan dog sitting like a statue in the corner of the examination room. "That's Gilda, a queen among dogs."

The dog's ears came forward at her name but she didn't move. It was like she was taking everything in and maybe judging a little.

"She seems very composed," Evie said.

"The best dog I've ever known, and I've known a lot." Finally he switched off the light, and pushed up his goggles. The rubber rim had left a red mark in the shape of a mask on his face. She focused on that, because it kept her mind from straying to his nice jawline and broad shoulders. "About the cat. Roberto, you said?"

She felt a flush start in her chest and move up. Why had she admitted to naming the cat when she wasn't keeping him? "Yes. How is he?"

"Other than being dehydrated and underfed, he's in decent shape overall. His temperament is remarkable. I've never had a cat just lie here and let me poke around an abscess." He pointed to his forehead. "Hence the eyewear. I've had more than a few cats go for my face."

"He's very calm. It must be because he's sick."

He shook his head. "It's the gingers. I call them cat-dogs. Even National Geographic agrees they're gregarious." Glancing at her hair, he added, "Hey, you match."

"Why, thanks. My brother said the same thing." Her voice was crisp and now the vet's face flushed. "Anyway, what do you think happened to the cat?"

He turned back to Roberto for another look. "It's an abscessed bite."

"From another cat? Or a vampire?"

The vet snorted very close to Roberto's ear and the cat looked at her reproachfully.

"Hard to say. We do have a few bloodsuckers in town, but you didn't hear it from me."

"Well, someone was mean enough to stick a wounded cat between my doors. I'm not impressed."

"You're sure it was closed when you left?"

"Quite sure." She perched on the plastic guest chair. "Anyway, how will you treat the bite?"

"I'm going to lance it and drain it," he said. "Normally I'd knock the cat out for it, but this guy is steady. I think I could try it with a local."

"I don't know... I don't want him to be in more pain than he already is."

"That's the beauty of abscesses. The moment they drain it brings relief. I'll dress the wound and you'll need to pill him for 10 days while it heals."

"Pill him? I can't keep him, Dr. Benson. Not with my allergies."

She hated seeing the disappointment come over his face. "I'm sorry to hear that," he said.

"If this cat is as amazing as you say, surely you can find him a good home."

"It's getting harder and harder, now that the city's talking about introducing regulations to keep cats indoors." Motioning for her to take over patting Roberto, he started gathering his equipment. "Maybe he ended up stuck in your door for a reason."

"I can't imagine what that would be. I just moved here." She ran her hand over the cat, carefully avoiding the wound. He rolled onto his good side and burst into a purr.

The motor was so loud the vet glanced over, and smiled. "He seems to have developed quite a fondness for you already. You must be a cat person."

"I'm not. In fact, I'm a pet skeptic." Pet phobic was more accurate, but no need to share that with a veterinarian.

His lip twitched. "Then you're in the wrong town, don't you think?"

"Quite possibly. But I'm going to make the best of it." Scratching under the cat's chin, she shook her head. "Don't waste your charm on me, pal. Find someone without allergies."

"Pardon me?" The vet stared at her.

"Not you," she said, flushing again. "Him."

A grin played on his face as he brought over a tray with rattling metal. "Can you hold him? My technicians have already gone home. Just scratch his head and talk to him."

She did as he asked. "Roberto, Roberto. How did you get stuck in my door?" She sneezed again.

"Good thing I've got goggles," the vet said, snapping them into place.

"Never mind his crappy jokes at my expense, Bertie-boo," she crooned. "Just grit your fangs and hold tight. It will all be over soon."

She watched as the vet shaved and disinfected the area, and then injected a local anesthetic. However, she looked away as he sliced into the wound. Her hands kept busy scratching and she hummed a little tune. Meanwhile she kept her eyes on the chart on the wall that featured 50 breeds of rabbits. She had no idea they came in so many colors.

Before long, the vet said, "It's okay. You can look now."

The wound was closed with a few neat stitches, and Roberto already looked brighter. His big green eyes scanned the room with new interest and settled on Gilda. Struggling for the first time, he slipped out of Evie's grasp, and when the vet nodded, she let him jump down. The cat walked over to the big dog with his tail high. He passed back and forth under her chin and stood up on his hind legs to brush Gilda's face. After a few minutes of this, Gilda rose and stretched, head down and hind end up.

"Play pose," the vet said. "She likes him."

The dog's hind end moved in a full circle, tail lashing, as the cat continued swishing under her chin. It was a riveting little cross-species ritual.

"Who wouldn't like him?" she asked. "I just wish I could keep him. It would mean life on allergy medication."

The vet nodded. "I'm assuming you want me to board him till he's well and then place him?"

"Please," she said, relieved. "I want him to have a good home."

Roberto left Gilda and did his figure eight between her shoes. He gave his purr-meow, clearly feeling much better.

"If I may..." the vet began. "This cat has already bonded with you, Evelyn."

"He's only known me three hours. I don't believe in insta-love."

The vet shrugged. "I'm just saying that this kind of attachment is unusual. Are you sure...?"

"I'm sure."

Stepping over the cat, she walked quickly to the door before he could talk her into taking him home. Gilda dodged to one side to get out of her path. Evie dodged at the same time and collided with a huge bag of dog food. There was a moment of pinwheeling arms and then she went down with a crash.

She had learned, through many similar accidents, to just stay still for a moment and make sure nothing was broken. Sometimes it was. She'd had a broken arm, finger and baby toe over the years, not to mention two concussions.

This time, when she opened her eyes, six startled eyes stared down at her. Gilda licked her ear, her brow furrowed in apparent worry. Roberto gave her a head butt, his purr at close range drowning out the vet's words. He was not taking no for an answer.

"I'm fine," she said. "It's just been a long day."

"You've got to watch your step around here," he said, taking her hands and pulling. "There's always something waiting to trip you up."

CHAPTER FOUR

E vie twirled around her kitchen in an erratic dance. "No, no, no."

Roberto was determined to accomplish his signature figure eight move between her feet, and she was equally determined to start her first day of work without being covered in orange cat hair. She'd chosen her outfit carefully —a black knit dress with some swing, a short black jacket with lots of buckles, black tights and black suede ankle boots. To her mind, it sent just the right message of big-city confidence and small-town fun. But she'd also chosen it without taking her houseguest into account—the one who ejected fur in clouds. He was a hazard to her wardrobe as well as her allergies.

"You're something else," she said, sidestepping him again on the way to the coffeemaker. "It's bad enough I have to show up at City Hall with puffy eyes and a chapped nose. Looks count in my line of work, you know."

Roberto gave a purr-meow that sounded rather flattering.

"Well, thank you. I know I'm nothing to sneeze at, figuratively speaking. But I've got a few strikes against me and this job is a big deal for me."

The cat's next mew had a question mark at the end. Never had she known a cat with a wider repertoire of vocalizations. It was almost as if he were talking, which is how she came to be having a conversation with a feline.

"There's a lot riding on it, Bertie-boo. Remember what Nick was teasing me about? No matter how hard I work, I keep getting fired. That's doing a number on my confidence. Not to mention leaving a guy behind in every city. This is my big do-over. My ninth life." She doled out a big helping of cat food and set it down. "Something tells me you've used up a few of yours, too."

He flicked his green eyes in seeming assent before digging into the food she set down. There was little of the typical feline delicacy about him. As the vet had said, he behaved much like a dog—at least in her limited experience of either species.

Shoving her arms through her coat sleeves, she said, "Okay, I'm off. Get some rest, okay? And wish me luck."

The cat didn't look up from his dish, and she slipped out the door with her stainless-steel coffee mug in one hand and purse in the other. On the porch, she set down the mug and pulled a roll of sticky tape out of her purse. She rolled the tape over her tights to pick up hair but strands had managed to embed themselves in the fabric, just like Roberto had insinuated himself into her life. It was all temporary, though. Dr. Benson had promised to keep an ear to the ground for the perfect home for the cat while he recovered. If all went well, she could transfer custody in a couple of weeks.

Dogs quickly pushed a certain cat out of her mind as she drove the short route from Riverdale to City Hall. Like most newcomers, she navigated the city by the huge bronze statues. Left at the Dalmatian outside the fire station. Right at the hospital's St. Bernard, and then parking in the public lot beside the new West Highland terrier. She shook her head at the last cocky statue. The dog had way too much attitude for the small space it inhabited. Soon there'd be no park without a bronze.

The sun came through the clouds as she paused in front of the menacing German shepherd outside City Hall. Was it a boy or a girl, she wondered? Not that she was an expert, but all the statues seemed genderless. Perhaps anatomically correct dogs were unseemly.

A breeze picked up her skirt and swirled it a bit as she climbed the stairs. There was warmth on the wind—a promise of spring—but the temperature dipped sharply as she walked through the double front doors of the old, gold brick building. The clock in the tower chimed twice, despite the fact that it was just before nine.

Someone buzzed her into the mayor's suite of offices and she stood in reception admiring the sleek oak panelling and leather guest chairs until a tall man came out of an office to the right. He was probably in his late thirties, just a few years older than she was, but his hair was already silvering. His eyes were blue, with crinkles at the corner, giving him the air of a young Paul Newman. It was a good thing she'd sworn off mixing business with pleasure years ago in her first political life, because he was exactly her type. And he wasn't wearing a ring. There was no harm in looking; unless she was much mistaken, he'd just done the same.

"Evelyn, welcome," he said. "Zeke Mackey, chief of staff. Your brother was singing your praises long before you moved here. He's one heck of a hockey player, although he plays pretty rough."

"Nick?" She was honestly surprised. "He's a pussycat."

Zeke led her into his office, grinning. "We don't talk about cats around here. It's all dog, all the time."

"Understood," she said, grinning back. "You do realize there's a fish on your wall?"

He glanced at a plaque that had a large gold fish affixed to it. "Trophy," he said. "My 16-pound salmon defeated your brother's measly trout."

"A proud moment indeed," Evie said, laughing. "So, what's the plan for my first day?"

"First up, a tour. Then a coffee."

"Sounds good," she said. "I'd love to check the place out."

As they walked through the halls of the old building, Zeke introduced her right and left and she struggled to file faces and names into their rightful place in her brain. Relationships were essential to her job, and remembering names was the critical first step to forging them.

Zeke pointed to a long row of portraits in the hall leading to the main entrance. Mayor Bradshaw's was last, and while the frame was the same size as the others, the portrait itself was a close-up, so his face looked bigger than everyone else's. He was a handsome man and he wasn't afraid to flaunt it. His painterly stylist had shaved off a good decade.

"You've joined us at an interesting time," Zeke said. "The office has taken some hits lately. I'm sure you've done your research, so I'll just confirm we're pulling back on dog court, but pressing forward on other initiatives that may cause tension."

"Such as?"

He peered over his shoulder before opening the door to the council hall. "Confidential, as yet. Suffice to say that you don't get to be the premier dog destination in the country without taking a few risks."

"Of course. But it's always good to let the dust settle. It's only been a few weeks since dog court shut down. Now's the time to build up goodwill. I was telling the mayor—"

"About the Easter egg hunt. I heard. Solid idea for community building. We're handing you the reins."

"Me? I'm not really an event planner, Zeke."

Ushering her into the center of the hall, he said, "In a small town we're forced to wear many hats. Besides, it's the perfect opportunity to get the lay of the land. You need to know the players, and they all come out for city events."

"Good point." She looked up at the domed ceiling. The founders had splashed out on the place long before the town showed promise of becoming anything special. "I look forward to getting out there and meeting people."

He took the big chair that would no doubt normally be the mayor's when Council was sitting. It had been reupholstered like a throne with red velvet cushions. Leaning back, he crossed his long legs with more grace than her brother could ever muster. His pant leg rode up and she saw a bruise and a few scratches.

"What happened there?" she asked.

He examined his leg briefly and shrugged. "I told you your brother played rough."

"Aren't you guys too old for games that leave you battered and bruised?"

"Never." The grin he gave her was impishly charming. "I'll never be too old for games and I bet Nick won't either."

"Boys." She shook her head as he got up and led her back into the main hallway.

"You like games too, or you wouldn't be in politics," he said. "But fair warning: people play rough in this town, too."

"It's a town for dog-lovers. How bad could it be?"

His ever-present smile dimmed a bit. "The mafia."

"Pardon me?"

"There's a group of supposed do-gooders that call them-selves the Rescue Mafia. They're behind several recent escapades that embarrassed this office. The mayor asked me to do what I can to suppress them, and in turn, I'm asking you."

"Suggestions?" she asked.

"Keep them busy and distracted. Leave them no time for trouble." He caught her arm before they walked into the cafeteria. "There are funds allocated for this project."

"The Rescue Mafia suppression project?"

He shushed her again. "They're standing in the way of civic progress. We've got new regulations coming down the pike and nothing can go wrong this time. The mayor's been perfectly clear: the threat needs to be neutralized."

Neutralized? Who talked this way outside of spy shows? She stared up at him wondering if he was serious. He had the kind of face that was always on the verge of a smirk.

"Why not bring them into the fold?" she said. "Treat them as valued stakeholders, and they're less likely to cause disruption."

"All chance of that ended when they staged a rally and desecrated the dog statues."

Now the grin returned and she grinned, too. The mafia and their buddies had placed acrylic knock-offs of the town's bronze collection in compromising positions. "I saw some of the photos," she said.

"They're always sneaking around," he said. "Hard to predict where they'll pop up next."

"At the Easter festival, no doubt, where I'll throw some golden rescue eggs their way."

He held open the door so she could walk ahead of him into the cafeteria. "I like you already, Evelyn. Your brother said you were the funny and smart one."

"Aw, how sweet," she said, passing in front of him. "Nick was always the pretty one."

Pouring coffee into a paper cup, he said, "Just a word of warning... the mayor doesn't particularly appreciate humor. He's a fine man and he's been like a father to me, but since he's discovered yoga and meditation, he's lost his funny bone."

She added cream and sugar to her coffee and pressed a lid onto the cup. "Smart is okay?"

"Smart is in the job description."

As they walked back to the mayor's suite, Zeke filled her in on some of the big events on the Dog Town social calendar. There were parades, pageants and parties, all of which celebrated dogs. It would be hard to make the Easter festival stand out.

"Don't look so worried," he said. "People really just want the same thing, only different. You don't need to stand out but fit in."

A beautiful woman with wavy dark hair was sitting in the waiting area when they got back. She was wearing a simple black suit with a cream sweater, but something about the cut and fit said expensive. The bag at her feet was obviously designer, but Evie never stayed on trend enough to know one logo from another.

The woman smiled up at Evie, and she returned it. She was trying to place the face when her boot collided with the designer bag. Her ankle turned, the coffee hit the floor with a pop and splash, and despite a valiant effort to regain her footing, she ended up splayed across the woman's lap.

"Oh my gosh, I'm so sorry," she said, thrashing as she tried to right herself. Zeke grabbed her under the armpits and hoisted her to her feet. Coffee covered the woman's taupe suede boots, and no doubt her pant legs.

The woman got to her feet, and actually laughed. "It's okay. Accidents happen."

That was some kind of accident. The bag hadn't been directly in Evie's path, but she had obviously gone off course admiring the woman's outfit. Still, sometimes it felt like fate was tossing her around like a ragdoll and laughing at the results.

"I'm Evelyn Springdale. Please let me pay for your dry cleaning." She stared down. "I hope your boots can be salvaged."

"It'll be fine," the other woman said. "I'm Hannah Pemberton. I'm sure the mayor will overlook the coffee stains."

"Hannah, it's such a pleasure to meet you," Evie said. "I just moved here and seeing your mother's art exhibit is already the highlight. I bought a couple of prints to frame."

Hannah's eyes lit up. "How kind of you to say. What do you do here?"

Zeke was plucking at Evie's sleeve but she forged ahead. "Public relations and event planning. Are you considering a move back to Dorset Hills?"

"Possibly. I'm looking for the right project to bring me home."

"Service dogs," Evie blurted.

Hannah tipped her head. "What about them?"

"Your mom had that series of sketches with service dogs.

It made me think that it would be a wonderful claim to fame if Dorset Hills became a service dog capital."

Zeke stepped forward to introduce himself. "No brainstorming at reception, Evelyn."

"I'd like to hear more," Hannah said. "Let's talk about it with the mayor."

"It's just you and Mayor Bradshaw today," Zeke said. "Evelyn and I have back-to-back meetings."

Evie retrieved the purse she'd kicked halfway across the office and placed it in Hannah's hands. "I think it survived unscathed."

Hannah reached into the side pocket, plucked out a card and offered it to Evie. "Since you're new in town, I've got a friend you should meet. She knows Dog Town inside out and is always willing to help. Text me and I'll connect you both."

"Wonderful. After such a rude introduction, you're too kind."

"Who knows," Hannah said. "Maybe it happened for a reason."

CHAPTER FIVE

The long stretch of property behind Dayton Manor was probably glorious in summer, but it was underwhelming in early spring. The manor itself was once the home of a Dorset Hills founding family. Dayton descendants had ultimately donated the property to the City, which hadn't figured out exactly what to do with it yet. As a result, it was one of the few spaces available for large events within city limits. Some brave purple and white flowers poked their heads up in the gardens and a bank of daffodils against the back wall would burst into bloom before long. Evie tried to imagine families foraging for Easter eggs among the gardens and statuary. There were at least two dozen stone figures of various shapes and sizes. There were solemn robed men that looked like wizards and mythological creatures that were vaguely—or overtly—threatening. It was an odd contrast to the quaint look the City had more formally adopted, and the likeliest reason the property hadn't been fully utilized.

"I was picturing something more festive," she said,

turning to Remi Malone, her companion on the scouting mission.

"It'll look great once the decorations go up," Remi said. "The City has everything we need to turn the place into a fabulous outdoor party setting. We can even put up tents if it rains."

Remi was a fundraiser for the hospital and Hannah Pemberton's friend. Hannah had barely left her meeting at City Hall before Remi had called reception, asked to speak to Evie, and offered to show her around town. Killing two birds with one stone, Evie had asked for help scouting locations. Two days later, they'd already visited four sites and she sensed Remi had saved the best for last, which was disappointing.

"What other options do we have?" she asked.

Remi was holding her beagle, Leo, like a baby in her arms. The dog was perfectly capable of walking but seemed to prefer being carted around. His long brown ears draped over Remi's sleeve as he stared at Evie, upside down. Even in that position she could tell he wanted to make friends. Well, she wasn't interested in canine friends. She had her fill of pets with the orange beast at home who was feeling so much better that he was scaling the cupboards and making constant lunges for the open door.

"Green space is limited in the city core," Remi said, shifting Leo's weight so that he was forced to sit up. "With the population growth, every square inch that can be developed is under construction."

Evie walked over to a tall stone centaur and patted its backside. "What about Rosetta Garret Gardens? It's closer to City Hall and there are mazes for the kids to run around."

"No dogs allowed," Remi said. "It's privately owned and they refuse to yield on that."

"Nothing else? I don't know what I was imagining, but this isn't it."

"It's the statues," Remi said, pointing to a five-foot faun standing on cloven feet. "They're quirky."

"Creepy, more like." Evie circled a winged creature that looked like a dragon with an old woman's face. "I'm going to see this one in nightmares."

Remi laughed. "Here, take this."

She tried to pass over Leo but Evie raised her hands. "Beagles shed, right? I'm allergic."

Leo gazed at Evie with reproachful eyes. She could tell this dog didn't hear "no" very often. Well, he could try, but his charm offensive wouldn't work on her.

Remi led the way past the biggest cluster of statues down toward the wooded area at the far end of the property. "Use your imagination," she said. "There will be potted flowers and shrubs, and streamers in purple, yellow and pink. We'll put rabbit ears on the scary statues so the kids don't cry."

A shiver ran down Evie's spine as they passed a sculpture that looked like a hippo with a rack of antlers. It was probably supposed to be whimsical but came across as macabre. Maybe if the day were sunny it wouldn't be so bad. "Don't you get bad vibes from this place?" she asked.

"No, but I have a shield." She clutched Leo to her heart. "Bad vibes can't penetrate fur. You should consider it, Evie. Sometimes you need armor against the crap in this town."

"Oh? How so?" She skirted what appeared to be a bipedal crocodile with pointy ears.

"Look around you. The Dayton family was eccentric and it seems to have been bred into us ever after. I'm speaking as someone born and raised here."

Evie stared up at the crocodile beast. "So you're saying there are monsters in the calm waters."

"That's exactly what I'm saying." Remi perched on the base of the statue, seemingly unconcerned about the talons under her backside. "I know you haven't been in the mayor's office long but I bet you've already been given a hit list."

Glancing down at her quickly, Evie fought a smile. "I guess a few people got on the mayor's bad side."

"Some would say he only has a bad side," Remi said. "Not me, obviously. As someone in the fundraising sector, I like everyone."

Everyone probably liked Remi, too. It was hard not to. Like her dog, she radiated kindness and good humor.

"I'm keeping an open mind," Evie said.

"Perfect. Because there are far more good people than bad in Dorset Hills."

"I believe you. Why else would my brother want to settle here?" She stared around despondently. "Are you really telling me this is the best site for the Easter festival?"

"I know this town inside and out and I've been involved in hundreds of public events. The pickings are slim."

"Maybe we could get water-soluble chalk or paint and let the kids decorate these creatures. That would be festive."

"Now you're talking," Remi said, standing. "Let me take some pictures and research what's safe for use on stone. Heaven forbid we permanently defile the Dayton collection."

Before Evie could protest, Remi thrust Leo into her arms and started digging around in her purse for her phone. Appraising Leo up close, Evie said, "He's pretty cute. I think it's the ears."

"It's the whole package," Remi said, snapping pictures

of a statue at close range. "That dog took me from a lonely introvert to the party queen you see today."

Leo lolled in Evie's arms and it looked like he wore a sly smile. He was winning her over and he knew it. White hairs stood out all over her navy peacoat.

When Remi's back was turned, she set Leo on the ground. He had paws and he might as well use them. The beagle began nosing around the gardens as they strolled across the rest of the vast property. Remi took dozens of photos to pitch the site to the City crew. It would be Evie's job to pitch it to the mayor's office and Zeke wasn't keen on any of the potential sites.

"Leo, what are you doing?" Evie said, watching dirt fly between his white paws. He didn't even pause, so intent was he on excavating a treasure in a flower bed filled with last season's dead foliage. She hurried over to stop him from getting completely filthy. It was too late for that, but she did manage to confiscate the object he'd unearthed.

Remi heard her gasp and looked over. "What'd he find?"

"Just a weird-looking rock," Evie said. "False alarm."

She pulled a plastic bag out of her purse, grabbed the knobby object, and slipped it into her pocket.

Leo looked up at her expectantly and she shook her head. There was no way she was giving him back that skull.

"WHAT KIND OF SKULL?" Nick asked, pouring pasta sauce into a pot and turning on the heat under it.

"I hoped you could tell me," she said. "You're the one who liked biology."

"Not that much," he said. "Do I want to see this before dinner?"

"It's just a bare bone by this point. No flesh, thank goodness." She had triple bagged the skull and pulled it out now. "Is it from a dog? Did Leo defile the Daytons' pet cemetery?"

He stared down at it, pondering. "Definitely not a dog. I can't place it at all. It's not like we have a lot of wildlife around here. Too much development." He nodded at his desk in the family room. "Leave it there and I'll do some research."

"Why would there be a skull from a strange animal in the garden of one of the founders?"

"There's probably some logical explanation," he said, turning the heat higher. He wasn't a patient cook, by any means. "Don't let your imagination run away on you."

"Have you been behind the Dayton manor? It's like a crazy gothic graveyard."

"See that?" He pointed the spoon toward the sliding back doors. "That's your imagination running away on you."

"Huh. And Zeke said I was the funny twin." She put the skull on his desk, then came back to the sink and washed her hands with plenty of soap.

He smirked as he stirred the sauce. "The cooties couldn't get through the double bagging."

"Triple. You can't be too safe." She stared at the sink full of dirty dishes and then the stinky sports equipment in the corner. There were muddy pawprints all over the cream tiles. How could two people who'd shared a very small space for nine months end up so different? "You need a housekeeper, brother."

"I don't like strangers touching my stuff," he said. "Which reminds me of a favor I need to ask. I just landed a contract in North Carolina, and I'll be gone for a couple of weeks. Could you look after—"

"Nick, I can't handle the dog." Clive, the big golden retriever, was sitting pretty by Nick's feet, watching him cook with a hopeful expression.

"What? I'd never leave Clive with you. I love this dog."

"What's that supposed to mean?"

He grabbed a pot of boiling pasta, carried to the sink and drained it. She stepped into his place at the stove and started stirring the sauce. Nick swore microwave ovens dried everything, but then he turned the heat so high it scorched the bottom unless you were on it constantly.

"No offence, Evie, but I doubt you could keep him alive. It's a lot of work looking after a dog."

"I could keep Clive safe. Not that I want to dog-sit. I'm just saying I'm capable."

He waggled his eyebrows before opening the dish-washer to grab some plates. She sincerely hoped they were clean. "You'll make a great mom someday, I'm sure."

"Just like you'll make a fabulous daddy." Her tone was equally mocking.

Raising a hand, he shuddered dramatically. "No kids for me, thank you very much." Dumping pasta from the pot onto two plates, he flicked a couple of pieces toward the dog. "Do you think mom wrecked us?"

Sighing, she turned off the burner. "Definitely. But let's not ruin our dinner. Better to talk about skulls."

"Agreed." He held out his plate and she carefully ladled tomato sauce over the pasta. "I assume you didn't mention the skull to Remi."

"Of course not. I got a strange feeling about it. Seemed best to keep it quiet." She set the pot on the already high pile in the sink and sat across from him.

"It's always best to keep things quiet around here," he said, with his mouth full. "That's one amazing beagle she's got, right?"

"How did you turn into this dog-lover?" she asked. "You used to be a pet skeptic like me."

"I still am, except for Clive." He nudged the dog with his foot. "He's got magic powers to soften the hardest heart."

It hadn't worked on Evie. At least, not yet. She found him intimidating, especially now, when he jumped to his feet, raced across the room and unleashed a volley of deep barks at the screen door.

Nick set down his fork, got up and walked over to the window. "Ev, there's something you've got to see."

She joined him, still chewing. On the back deck sat Roberto, with his tail coiled neatly around his paws. The ragged left ear and rainbow-colored collar and tag she'd put on him were instantly recognizable. "How the—?" She fumbled with the latch. "Get in here, you."

The cat sauntered past her with his tail in the air. Clive took a little lunge at him and Roberto stepped sideways before proceeding to do his figure eight between Nick's feet.

"You can't leave your cat to wander, Evie," he said, stooping to pat Roberto. "The City's cracking down on outdoor cats. Besides, he's not fully healed yet."

"First, he's not my cat. Second, I didn't leave him out. He was eating his dinner in the kitchen when I left the house after work."

"Well, first, he thinks he's your cat. He covered three blocks looking for you, including a busy intersection. And second, if he got out, we better go check your place to make sure it's secure."

She shook her head, confused. "Let's finish up and drive over." They sat down again, but she didn't pick up her fork.

Her appetite had faded with concern that someone had broken into her house and left the door open. "What did you want to ask me to do, by the way?"

"Just bring in the mail." His ready grin reappeared. "Think you can handle that?"

Roberto shifted his attention to Clive, who seemed quite fascinated by the various figure eight combinations between his paws. "I'm less sure of that than I was 10 minutes ago. Things aren't adding up today."

Shoving the last of the pasta into his mouth, Nick mumbled, "Just watch your back like I told you until I'm back for Easter, okay? Let sleeping dogs lie."

CHAPTER SIX

She'd overdressed. The word "gala" on the flyer Zeke had handed her about the hospital fundraiser had been misleading. Now she was the only one wearing sequins in a room where there were plenty of lumberjackets and some fringed leather. Her favorite dress, with a glittery bodice and floaty skirt in deep purple, had never let her down before. Tonight it stood out like a hand-painted Easter confection in a carton of regular white eggs. The location—the new legion hall—probably should have been a tip-off, but still... gala wasn't a word you used for a gathering in a men's club that featured stuffed deer heads on the wall.

"You look gorgeous," Remi said, giving her a hug. "Are you going somewhere after?"

Evie nodded. "I have a thing. I can't stay too long." She sincerely hoped Remi wouldn't inquire further since she probably knew about local black-tie events.

Remi herself was wearing taupe pants and a cream cashmere sweater, no doubt to hide some of the hair blown out by her beagle companion. Leo was on his paws for a change, working the crowd solo. "I'm so glad you came," she said. "There are people I want you to meet."

"You've had a great turnout," Evie said, following Remi through the crowd.

"Thankfully. You have no idea how hard it is to come up with new ways to get people to open their wallets for the hospital foundation. But I never give up."

The theme of the evening was "Spring Fever," and there were so many pots of flowers that the place smelled like a funeral home. Or maybe that was the stuffed deer heads. Evie flinched. It felt like they were staring down at her with reproachful, glassy eyes. Surely people didn't hunt in the surrounding hills and mount their kills. These must be old and dusty relics.

Remi followed her gaze. "I know. I tried to get the brotherhood to take them down for the gala but they refused. They're still mad at the mayor for taking over their old hall and turning it into headquarters for the Canine Correction Department. The deer heads are part of making the new place their own."

"It just seems odd for a pet-friendly town to celebrate hunting," Evie said.

"*Dog* friendly," Remi corrected. "The current regime isn't so friendly to other animals."

"Or even dogs," another voice said. "The current regime is a farce."

Remi shook her head and smiled. "Cori. At least let me introduce you before climbing on your soapbox."

"I don't need a soapbox," Cori said, glaring at Remi and then transferring the look to Evie.

The petite, dark-haired woman might actually need a soapbox to make herself seen, but certainly not heard. Her clear, confident voice carried and others turned to look at her.

"Evelyn, allow me to introduce my friends," Remi said. "They're all very nice, with one small exception."

Cori muttered something under her breath that sounded like "suck-up traitor." Another woman—with a black dog at her side—pulled Cori backwards. Evie sensed the tall woman was the official leader, but there were probably lots of checks and balances in this group. They seemed to prickle with energy, ready to explode into action at a second's notice.

Remi introduced them one by one. All the women were attractive. All were casually dressed. The only one who even wore a skirt was Andrea MacDuff, or "Duff," a real estate agent who had a head of sleek auburn hair that was everything Evie wished her own hair could be. It was funny how a slightly different shade and curls could be the difference been geek and chic.

Bridget Linsmore was tall, fair and as composed as the feathery black dog at her side. He looked like he was assessing everyone in the room and transmitting his findings to Bridget through the fingertips resting on his head.

"Bridget runs a successful dog rescue and showcases her work at the famous Thanksgiving Rescue Pageant," Remi said.

Ah. She'd guessed right: Rescue Mafia member numero uno. "A pleasure to meet you," Evie said. "I've heard about you and can't wait for your next pageant."

Remi's quick recap of her friend's names and accomplishments tested Evie's excellent memory skills. There was Mim Gardiner, the nurse, Nika Lothian the vet technician, Arianna Torrance, a dog breeder who looked like an angel, Sasha Wildwood and Maisie Todd, both dog groomers, and

Flynn Strathmore, the famous cartoonist. All of the women were likely in their early to mid thirties. They gave off a warm friendly vibe, as if they'd been friends forever. She wouldn't have been surprised to see them link arms and strut through the room like schoolgirls.

Then there was Cori Hogan. She was petite and dark, with an Audrey Hepburn look, but there was nothing fragile about her. She was wearing jeans and a grey hoodie.

"Nice dress," Cori said, smirking.

"Cori!" It was Duff, evidently the Mafia PR manager.

"What? It *is* a nice dress. For some event, somewhere. Just not the Dog Town legion hall."

"Cori." This time it was Bridget and her calm voice seemed to hold more weight than Duff's, because Cori shrugged. "I apologize for Cori's manners," Bridget said. "She's great with dogs but forgets the niceties sometimes."

"You look lovely, Evelyn, truly," Duff said. "Cori's hostile to all government representatives. It's not personal."

"Understood," Evie said. "What do *you* do, Cori?"

"Fight for the underdog. Literally." Cori put her hands on her slim hips. "I heard you were hired as a fixer after Sasha embarrassed the mayor enough to disband dog court."

"You give me too much credit," said Sasha, a pretty blonde with a ready smile. "One litter of pups can't bring down a regime."

"It was a start," Cori said. "And now there's a fixer to rebuild the circus."

Evie smiled. "I'm no ringmaster. I'm just here to do some public relations for the City."

Cori's eyebrows swooped together like delicate swallows. "You don't even like dogs."

"Who doesn't like dogs?" Evie scoffed. "Why would I move here if I didn't like dogs?"

"Because you're desperate to salvage your rep?" Cori said. "Sasha has friends in San Fran. They said you got fired from your last job and came here to recover because it would be the last place anyone would look for a dog-hater."

Sasha winced and then mouthed, "Sorry."

Evie was no stranger to aggressive tactics but the strength of Cori's attack surprised her. However, she'd long since learned to stand up to bullies, even petite, dog-loving bullies.

"Cori, you're every bit as combative as I'd heard," she said. "Although no one said you were mean."

"I'm not—"

"Yeah, you are," Evie said. "There's no reason for a personal attack. I can only assume you're jealous of my dress."

Everyone broke out in a laugh and even Cori's mouth twitched. "Unlikely. I haven't worn a frock like that since prom."

"You went to prom?" Duff asked. "I figured you were above such frivolous things."

"Not always. But I've matured, unlike some people." She eyed Evie again. "What *are* you doing in Dog Town, anyway?"

"Well, you're right about my getting the boot from my last job. I didn't do what they wanted me to do when they wanted me to do it. But you're wrong about my hating dogs. I'm just allergic to animals." Leo wove through many legs and appeared beside her stilettos. It was as if he sensed she needed him. She scooped the dog up and he instantly went limp, basking in the attention. "I certainly like this one."

Cori snorted. "Leo doesn't count. Everyone likes Leo."

"First kind words I've heard from you about Leo," Remi said.

"You coddle him like an infant and let him get away with murder, but that doesn't mean he isn't a good dog," Cori said. "There are no bad dogs... just bad owners."

Remi turned to Evie. "Feel better? Cori's always tearing a strip off someone. But there is no better advocate for dogs in this city."

"Country," Cori corrected.

Everyone laughed again.

"I heard that, too, believe it or not," Evie said. "Do you train service dogs, Cori?"

"Of course. Why?"

"I'm interested in exploring how the City can build more of a reputation in that area."

"Good idea," Remi said. "It would be on-brand for Dorset Hills."

"What does the mayor say?" Bridget asked.

Evie grinned. "Haven't asked him yet. I'm just curious."

"A distraction," Cori said. "You want to throw money at something positive so people stop looking at the negative."

"What's wrong with throwing money at service dogs?" Evie asked. "Seems like there are worse causes."

Cori got a little closer, staring up at Evie with fierce eyes that were as dark and shiny as a crow's. "Whatever you're scheming, there's something you need to know."

Evie held her ground. "And what's that?"

"I cannot be bought." She gestured at her friends. "They cannot be bought."

Duff laughed. "Speak for yourself, Cori. I can totally be bought for the right cause."

"Service dogs," Sasha said. "I'm open to hearing ideas. You know I want to train Tuni to go into service."

"I already have a therapy dog, so I'm all ears," Remi said.

Cori glared at them. "I hate you guys."

"You love us," Bridget said. "And we love you. But if the city is throwing money at something positive for service dogs, I'm hearing them out."

"Better to be an advisor on the ground floor," Duff said. "If Evelyn's recruiting, she'd do well to have the best trainer in the country on board."

Evie only noticed that Cori was wearing gloves now, as she flipped the bird at Duff. The middle finger of the knit gloves was neon orange.

"Fine," Cori said. "I'm happy to consult with you, as long as you take us all as a package deal."

"Sounds good. The committee is convened."

"As long as the mayor agrees," Remi reminded her.

"True enough," Evie agreed, handing Leo back to his rightful owner. A few sequins had fallen off her dress when he squirmed and now they glittered in his fur.

"You're aware that we'll make you suffer if you're stringing us along?" Cori asked.

"I would expect no less," Evie said.

Cori's feathers seemed to settle suddenly and she stepped back into the ranks of her friends. "You know what else I heard about you through my contacts?"

Evie steeled herself. "Dying to know."

"That you got fired for being soft."

The shot pierced Evie's armor but triggered her fake smile to switch on at the same time. "What a terrible thing to say."

"Yes and no." Cori's arms were crossed and both orange flipping fingers showed. "Soft means you're redeemable. We'll give you enough leash to see if you—"

A chorus of voices drowned Cori's last words.

"I've got to go, Remi," Evie said. "I'm heading to a cock-tail party over in Pemsville."

Remi followed her to the door, apologizing profusely for Cori all the way. "She's got a good heart, trust me. It's just that true dog lovers and advocates have really been burned lately. It'll take time to earn back some trust."

"I know," Evie said, slipping her arms into the sleeves of her coat. There was still white dog hair all over it from their site visits two days earlier, despite her thorough application of the lint roller. "Zeke tried to vote down Easter at the Dayton estate, by the way, but the mayor liked the idea, so we're good to go."

"Yay!" Remi said. "Sorry about the dog hair. And I should have texted to say the event was casual."

Evie thought about carrying on the ruse but gave up. "Maybe I'll meet a hot guy on the way home and the dress won't be wasted."

"Stick around. There are hot guys here, too."

"Cori sucked the party out of me," Evie said. "But I'll come back strong. I always do."

CHAPTER SEVEN

It was almost nine when Evie pulled into her driveway, and dusk had fallen hard over the city, like a black drop cloth. San Francisco had never seemed so dark, but she was probably glamorizing it in her memory. It wasn't like she had been particularly happy there, or in Seattle before that. There was always the sense that she wouldn't be around long so there was no point getting attached. This time, with Nick nearby, she hoped it would be different. Dorset Hills may not be the forever home she'd envisioned, but it felt like time to set down some roots.

A dark shape flitted across the driveway and up the front stairs. She choked back a little scream. It was just a cat. She knew it couldn't be Roberto because Nick had found and blocked the small gap in the basement crawl space that the cat had obviously used to escape the other day.

She started up the stairs and the motion light came on. "Go away, kitty, the inn is full."

The cat pulled back into the shadows as she unlocked

the door. "I'm serious," she said. "One cat is all I can handle. More than I can handle, in fact."

She pushed the door open and turned to check on the lurking cat. There was a sudden flash as it darted past her into the house. "Hey! You come back here."

Reaching for the light switch, she saw Roberto's backside as he trotted into the kitchen.

"Are you kidding me?" she called after him. "How the heck did you get out of this house?" Nick had combed the house inside and out with her and found no other point of exit. The cat must be able to fold himself into a sheet of paper and slide under the door. "Roberto, stop. I'm talking to you. Our agreement was that I feed you and shove pills down your throat and you lay low till you're fully recovered. What part of that didn't you understand?"

The orange cat kept walking, and she noticed his tail, normally flying high, was low and twitching. In fact, his posture was completely different. He seemed to be laboring. Worry replaced anger, and she hurried after him. "Are you all right, Bert?"

He turned and her breath caught in her throat. The cat was carrying something. At first she hoped it was a brown furry hat, but the way it swung in his jaws told her it had bones, not seams.

"Drop it," she said. "Drop it!"

Roberto didn't drop it. Instead, he set the brown furry thing gently on a white tile, where it lay, unmoving.

Evie screamed for real this time and cut it off with a hand over her mouth. The brown thing was a rodent, the biggest she'd ever seen. It was either a mutant rat or another species entirely. She held back, waiting to see if it moved. Roberto was staring at it, likely doing the same. When nothing happened, he leaned down and started licking the creature, scraping his rough tongue over its head.

"Ugh, don't. It's loaded with parasites, Roberto. Leave it. I'll—I'll do something with it."

Roberto continued to groom his trophy as she tiptoed across the kitchen on stilettos. Suddenly the creature wriggled. Evie lunged backwards, lost her balance and stumbled into the counter. Putting both hands behind her, she pushed off and hoisted herself onto the laminate surface. Her heels dangled and clacked into the cupboard below.

"Oh my gosh, it's alive. You've brought a big rat in here alive. You're disgusting."

He raised a paw and placed it on the creature before looking up at her. His ears were back and his tail lashed. It almost seemed like he was as disgusted by her as she was by him.

"What? You expect me to be proud of you for escaping and bringing that thing in here? Now what are you going to do—chase it around and murder it?"

His tail lashed faster, snap-snap, and then he went back to licking his catch. What was he doing? Softening it up for the kill? She knew cats often played with their prey but not that they groomed it like that. He was treating it as if it were a kitten. It was actually much bulkier than a kitten and he'd struggled to carry it.

She lifted her legs, spun around on the counter and dropped onto the floor on the other side to pick up the purse she'd dropped, all the while keeping her eye on the rodent. Plucking out her phone, she called Nick.

"Just heading onto the rink," he said. "Can I call you back?"

"No, it's urgent, Nick. The cat—"

"Anything to do with the cat can wait till my game's over."

She hopped up on the counter again and spun back around to face the cat and his trophy. "It can't, honestly. He's brought something into the house."

"Brought something in? You mean he escaped again? Ev, you're going to have to hire a contractor to check the house from top to bottom. That place is a dump. I don't know why you didn't rent a nice condo."

"I'll get someone in. In the meantime, he caught this big rodent and—"

"Evie. I don't want to know what he's doing with a dead rodent."

"But it's *not* dead. That's the point. And it's lying on my kitchen floor."

There was a loud sigh at the other end. "Remember how you used to save mice that got into the house when we were kids? Just do the same thing. Put a shoebox over top, slide cardboard underneath and then carry it outside."

"I used to be braver. And the rodents used to be smaller. This thing has to weigh more than a pound."

"You're exaggerating." His voice was strained, and she guessed he was lacing his skates. "Even a rat doesn't weigh that much."

"It's not a rat. I don't know what it is. I'll take a picture and—"

"Evie, you know I'm not big on rodents, either. Mom put the fear in both of us. So, just take it outside and let it go back where it came from."

"I think it's injured. Roberto is grooming it."

"Grooming it?" He paused and then made a decision. "No. I am not forfeiting my game to deal with your cat's treasure. I need to blow off some steam before leaving tomorrow."

"He's not my cat. Now more than ever he is not my cat."

"Locking up my phone, now. You'll handle this, sis. You're not the shrinking violet you make yourself out to be."

"I am, though. I am that shrinking violet when there's vermin in my house."

"You're used to rats. You work in politics." He laughed at his own joke. Someone shouted his name and it sounded like Zeke. "Gotta go, Evs. Good luck with the vermin."

Roberto stopped grooming and stared up at her. His ears came forward, and it was like he was entreating her to do something. Well, she'd have to do something. The situation wasn't resolving itself. Easing herself down from the counter, she tiptoed past them and into the office. There was a stack of shoeboxes in a corner that hadn't made their way upstairs. She tipped out a pair of boots. Then she grabbed a larger box, and ripped it apart as she walked back to the kitchen.

Roberto had draped his orange striped body over the rodent. She wasn't sure if he was keeping it still, keeping it warm or protecting it from her. Regardless, she had to take over now.

"Okay, back away," she said. "Let's get this thing out of here."

When he didn't move, she fanned him with the cardboard. "Bert, I mean it. Let me take care of it."

Now she nudged him with her stiletto and he backed away reluctantly. Leaning down, she stared at the creature. It was an odd-looking thing, with a rectangular head. "Maybe it's in the mink family," she said. "Or a chinchilla. What do chinchillas look like? Maybe someone's raising them for fur coats."

The creature scrabbled to roll over and she stepped back. When she saw its bare pink tummy, she realized it was just a baby. What had appeared to be a huge rat was a small something else. It was very much alive, and judging by the squeaking sounds, it missed its mother.

"Oh no," she said. "I can't just dump it outside now. It's a baby, Bert. You stole a baby."

Now that she knew it couldn't run too far, she knelt beside it and examined it. The fur was reddish brown and bristly—not likely coveted for coats.

There were no puncture wounds on the creature that she could see. Wherever the cat had found it, he apparently hadn't harmed it at all. He'd carried or dragged it here by the scruff. She had no idea why, but he was now parading about with his tail high and seeming quite proud of himself. He dropped a constant stream of small mews, as if he were telling the whole story. Too bad she didn't speak feline.

"I have no idea what you're saying," she told him. "But pets can't have pets. And this one may die without his mother."

She got up and lined the shoebox with paper towels and then put on rubber gloves. After setting the box carefully over the mewling baby, she gently slid the flat piece of cardboard underneath and tipped the box over. When all was still, she swapped out the flat board for the shoebox lid. Standing, she gently poked some holes in the lid and slid a big elastic band around the box. She added twine for good measure. There was no way this thing would be running around her car.

"Let's go," she said. "You're coming with me to explain what happened."

She walked toward the front door, with Roberto close

behind. His tail was high and his purr loud enough to hear over her clicking heels.

Opening the door, she said, "Nick was right. I only want to deal with political rats, Roberto. When this is over, you and I are going to have a sit-down. The arrangement we have simply isn't working."

His next meow had a distinct edge to it.

"Don't talk back to me," she said, locking the door behind them. "Let's just get this done."

CHAPTER EIGHT

D r. Benson's tired blue eyes opened wide when Evie walked into the clinic. Her coat hung open and her dress had drooped in ways it was not designed to do. A cool breeze across her cleavage prompted her to pinch the two sides of her coat closed with her free hand. The other clutched the shoebox to her abdomen.

"You look very nice," he said. "I hope everything is okay with Roberto. I could barely understand you on the phone. It sounded like you were driving fast."

"With a cat trying to grab the wheel," she said. "Oh. Where is he?"

The door had closed with Roberto outside. He sat in the darkness, eyes glowing, and his mouth opened in a complaint.

Evie elbowed the door open while juggling the box and keeping her dress G-rated. "Get in here and tell the doctor what you did. After he saved your life, and all."

"It wasn't quite that dramatic," the vet said. "Abscesses are fairly routine in cats. How is he doing?"

Roberto sauntered across the waiting room to greet

Gilda first. The big dog lowered her front end into a play pose, then spun in a quick circle and repeated the move. Roberto head-bumped her on either side of her long muzzle and collapsed between her front paws. She poked his spotted belly with her nose and he batted her gently.

"Huh," Dr. Benson said. "Gilda's good with cats but I've never seen her take such a shine to one in particular. He's quite unique."

"He's Houdini in fur. My brother sealed up the only hole we could find in the house the other day, and Roberto managed to escape again. Tonight he brought home a friend." She looked down at the box, which had been suspiciously quiet. "I think it's some kind of rat. A big one."

"Let's take a look," he said, turning to go into an examination room. "Did he injure it?"

"I couldn't see any wounds." She watched her feet as Gilda and the cat capered in front of her. "It looked like a baby, but I'm certainly no expert."

"Rat pups can fit in the palm of your hand."

"Then maybe it's a guinea pig."

"Again, they're pretty small. Now I'm really curious."

She set the box on the stainless-steel examination table, and retreated till her back hit the door. If the inhabitant of the box made a break for it, she was ready to bolt. Meanwhile, Roberto jumped onto the examination table beside the box.

Lifting him down, the vet said, "I don't think so, pal. I didn't come out at this time of night to lose a patient to you."

"I'm sorry for bringing you out," Evie said. "I couldn't just leave it outside, like my brother suggested. I'm no fan of rodents, but I can't stand to see something suffer." She thought about what Cori had said earlier in the evening.

"No wonder I got fired from my last job for being too soft. Or so says the Dog Town rumor mill."

He made a dismissive sound as he pulled the twine and elastic bands off the shoebox. "Who cares about Dog Town gossip? Having a good heart is a plus in my books."

"Not so much in political jobs," she said. A flush started somewhere in the vicinity of her ribcage and rushed north. His smile was enough to tell her he hadn't left his home at this hour simply to benefit a rat in need. She blinked a few times, reminding herself that he was too nice a man to endure whatever curse plagued her romantic life. Dog Town and her current job could be just a memory by this time next year, anyway.

His curious expression changed to shock when he lifted the lid of the shoebox. "Oh. Not a rat. Definitely not a rat."

"Well? What is it?"

Snapping on rubber gloves, he lifted the creature and turned it. Then he examined its paws. "It *is* in the rodent family. And you're correct it's a pup. Given the webbed feet, I could make an educated guess, but I'd like to confirm first."

He put the pup back in the box, fitted the lid over it, and turned to his laptop. As he clicked the keys, Roberto jumped back on the table and draped himself over the box.

"Bertie, off. It's out of your paws, now," Evie said.

Ignoring her, the cat kneaded the cardboard gently with his claws and fixed his eyes on Jon's back. The vet straightened, almost as if he could feel the gaze, and when he turned, he did a double take. "This cat is really something."

"He certainly is. What did you find?"

"What you've got here is a capybara pup. Just a day or two old, I would guess."

"A capybara? What's that?"

"A member of the rodent family indigenous to Brazil. People call them giant guinea pigs. In fact, this little lady might grow to be 150 pounds."

She stared at him, trying to figure out what this meant. "What is a giant guinea pig from Brazil doing in Dorset Hills? And a baby, yet? It's barely spring. Surely they're not reproducing in this weather."

The vet leaned back against the counter and crossed his arms. "There's zero chance she was bred in the wild. It was a very cold winter, and her parents wouldn't have survived."

"Well, is there a zoo I don't know about?"

"The only zoo closed 20 years ago. Exotic animals like this are illegal in Dorset Hills. And the entire state."

"Then... what's going on?"

He gestured to the chair. "Evie, have a seat."

"I'm fine, just tell me," she said.

His brow creased and his frown deepened. "I can't be certain, of course, but it's possible there's an exotic pet ring in Dorset Hills."

Evie's fingers reached for the back of the chair and the vet took two quick steps and pressed her shoulders till she sat down.

"A pet ring?" she said. "As in, someone's buying and selling rare animals?"

He shrugged. "Or just a hobbyist and collector of exotics. I can't think of any other explanation."

"But aren't exotic pets more like white tigers?"

"It can be any animal rare enough that people are willing to pay for it. Capybaras aren't endangered anymore, but they're probably a prize in some circles."

She covered her face with her hands. "Oh no no no. Mayor Bradshaw will lose his new cool if he finds out we have an exotic pet ring. And that my cat—the cat I'm not supposed to have—exposed it. What are the chances?"

"It will be a first to my knowledge," Jon said.

Staring up at him through her fingers, she said, "I was hired to fix problems in Dog Town, not create them."

"You didn't create this problem, Evie. It existed before you arrived and you uncovered it. Wouldn't that make you a hero in the mayor's eyes?"

Roberto strutted to the end of the stainless-steel table and bumped his head against the vet's back as if to say, "I'm the real hero here."

Evie sighed. "Uncovering a problem doesn't make me a hero. *Fixing* it does."

"Well, you'll disclose it to the Canine Corrections Department and they'll get the to bottom of it. You're still fixing it."

She shook her head. "The story will get out and it'll reflect badly on Dog Town. Everything gets blown out of proportion here."

It was the vet's turn to sigh. "Tell me about it. I miss the varied practice I used to have. The City's relentless favoritism for dogs is pushing every other animal out of town."

"Or underground."

"I would never encourage exotic pets, no matter what. It takes an expert to care for rare animals properly. This pup needs its mother, and a heat lamp, for starters."

"What else?" Evie said, getting out her phone to take notes.

He shook his head. "You'd better not be thinking what I think you're thinking."

"Is it healthy?" she asked.

Opening the box, he examined it more closely. He

pulled gently on its scruff until it let out a loud squeak that brought Roberto running. The cat leaned around the vet's hand and licked the capybara pup.

Pushing the cat away, Dr. Benson said, "She's responsive and not dehydrated, so at the moment she's stable. But things can turn very quickly with young animals that have been taken from their mothers."

"It must have been with its mom until very recently, then. Do you think it was left outside?"

"I doubt it. There are no signs of exposure and it's a cool evening. Besides, it's too valuable to the breeder."

He put the pup back in the box, and before he could replace the lid, Roberto draped himself over the opening. The pup instinctively moved toward the warm body. A roaring purr began.

"It's like he thinks he's its mom," she said.

Jon studied the cat. "I've seen dogs behave like nannies, but seldom cats. Still, he clearly has no plans to do it harm."

"Is that why he took it? To play nanny?"

The vet stroked the cat's back and the purring revved even higher. "I have no idea how a capybara arrived home in your cat's jaws. It's baffling." Stripping off his latex gloves, he pulled his phone out of his back pocket. "Let's call the CCD."

"No," she said quickly. "I'll handle this."

"Evie, you can't care for this pup. Without its mom, it'll need to be bottle fed every couple of hours."

"Bottle fed? Baby formula?"

"Specialized animal formula. With an eyedropper."

"But with this formula and a heat lamp, it would be fine for a day or two until I can reunite it with its mom?"

He shook his head. "No. I will not be part of this. I'm obligated to report sick animals to the City."

"You said yourself it's not sick." She got up and walked over to him. "Jon, I just need a bit of time to figure out where it came from. Then I'll report it quietly and we'll disband the operation before anyone hears about it."

He held up his hand. "Look, Evie. I'm no fan of Bill Bradshaw or his policies. In fact, if I hadn't committed to long-term clients, I'd have moved to Pemsville by now. I need to report this because my first priority is animal welfare."

"All I'm asking for is a day or two to figure this out myself." She clutched his sleeve. "There's a very good chance I'll lose my job over this if you call it in now."

"Why on earth would they fire you?"

"Because they hired me to solve PR problems, not create them. And Jon, I've been fired eight times for far less. It's wearing me down. So, I'm asking you... please?"

Roberto left the capybara and jumped down so he could weave a figure eight between their legs. It felt like he was trying to bring them to harmony, but she was probably giving the cat too much credit.

"I promise I will take good care of it," she said.

"How can you take care of it? They're crepuscular."

She blinked a few times, knowing it was a test. "That is what Google is for."

"No. If you're dead set on finding the breeder yourself, I will keep the pup here."

"But you have staff. They'd be so excited about the rare baby the news would leak. Could you take it home?"

He shook his head. "Tenants downstairs."

"Then just give me two days," she said. "I'm quite sure I can find out who has the capy-mama. It can't be that easy to hide a 150-pound guinea pig. By that time, I'll figure out how to solve the problem without raising any political trouble."

Gilda came to the vet's side, as if she knew Jon needed her. His right hand reached absently for her ears and scratched them. "Capybaras mature quickly. She has teeth already and will be running around and chewing things very soon. These animals are as intelligent and trainable as a dog and even more social. They get extremely anxious when left on their own."

She ran her hand over Roberto's back and he arched to meet it. "Now it's time to earn your keep, buddy. You're up for nanny."

The cat went back to the box and collapsed against it, purring and kneading the air. The vet tickled his spotted tummy and Roberto grabbed his hand and pretended to attack.

She knew the cat was wearing him down with cuteness, and sure enough, Jon soon left the exam room to collect the formula and eyedroppers she'd need.

"What a great cat," he said, when he got back. "You're lucky he found you."

Evie buttoned her coat and reached for her purse, now bulging with supplies. "He's not staying, Jon. This cat could cost me my job."

"That's life in politics, right? You need a thick skin as well as a tough heart."

"Two fatal flaws," she said, lifting the cat. He snuggled under her chin and his paws collapsed neatly, like a folding chair. He didn't want to leave under his own steam. "I can't carry you *and* your rat baby, Bertie. On your pins."

She set the cat down and when she stood, Jon was staring at her. "There's something special about your connection to this cat."

Brushing cat hair from her face with a coat sleeve equally covered in cat hair, she sneezed three times in rapid succession. "That's *with* allergy medication. I'm afraid it won't work in the long term."

Roberto's eyes narrowed as he stared up at her and his ears flattened. But then he turned his attention on Gilda. The big dog leaned down and licked his head, her tail waving gently.

"I'll be in touch tomorrow," Jon said. "I want regular reports on the capybara or I'm extracting her."

"Understood," she said, sliding the elastic band over the box. "And appreciated."

She was tired and overwhelmed, but his hand on her shoulder as he guided her out felt warm, comforting and oddly heavy. He accompanied her to the car and opened the door, laughing when Roberto hopped into the driver's seat.

"See what I mean?" she asked. "Thinks he's in charge."

She turned to get into the car, stumbled on a pebble, and staggered into the vet. He caught her with both hands. "Easy now. You must be tired."

"I am," she said. If only she could blame fatigue for every awkward stumble.

He leaned in once she was seated, and Roberto crawled into her lap. "What a perfect pair," he said. "I know one when I see one."

"So not perfect." She tried to push the cat off her dress. Her face was warm again but she wouldn't give in to foolish hormones. Jon was the nicest man she'd met in years, and he deserved better than her crazy life. The way things were going, she'd be gone before long. No one with allergies should set down roots in a pet-crazy city anyway. But she looked up at him as she started the car and wished things might have been different. "Thanks, Jon. Goodbye."

CHAPTER NINE

Evie glanced up at the bronze German shepherd as she raced through Bellington Square and shook her head over how much life had changed. Just six weeks ago she'd head down to Fisherman's Wharf in the morning to gulp coffee and fresh sea air before work. The barking sea lions offshore didn't have the menace of this towering dog statue that was going to demolish her ninth life. Then where would she go? It was a big country, but not so big that news of her failings hadn't reached the ears of dog trainers in Dorset Hills. Now she had a giant guinea pig baby in her bathtub, being nannied by the cat who'd adopted her. It was as surreal as this crazy town.

"Oh good, you're here," said Chloe, the receptionist, as Evie rushed into the office. "I was getting worried."

"Sorry," she said. The big clock over the reception desk read 9:04. Worrying about four minutes seemed excessive, but she'd never once been late in San Francisco, and she couldn't afford to squander goodwill here. Not so soon. Not when there was an illegal exotic animal in her home that needed to be fed frequently. Luckily, the little one had taken quickly to the formula during her middle-of-the-night feedings.

"The beagle people are waiting in the big boardroom. Zeke said you'd take the meeting."

"The beagle people?"

Chloe nodded. "I think they said beagles." She beckoned and when Evie leaned in, she whispered, "It's a tough crowd. They were sniping at each other."

"Where's Zeke?" Evie asked, checking her phone for texts and finding none.

"He left with the mayor for a meeting. Seemed urgent."

It must have been urgent indeed to disrupt the mayor's mindfulness hour. He blocked off eight to nine every morning for silent reflection.

Evie took off her jacket and stowed it in the closet. "Okay, but he didn't send me any intel about these beagle people."

"I guess he figured you'd wing it. It's always one breed group or another. The golden retriever people are the loudest."

"Loudest?"

Chloe shrugged, plugging her earbuds back in. "Every group thinks its breed is special but the golden retriever people are entitled, if you ask me."

The boardroom door opened and a woman with brown corkscrew curls stuck her head out. She was wearing a blue and black lumberjacket, jeans and work boots. "We're waiting for the mayor," she said. "Some coffee would be nice, too."

"Coffee, of course. Chloe, do you mind?"

Chloe did mind, but she left it at a discreet eye roll. "I'll text when it gets here," she said, after the woman retreated to the boardroom. "That's Leann Cosgrove, by the way. Also entitled."

Evie straightened her shoulders and summoned a smile. Stakeholder meetings were nothing new, even if the subject matter was.

"Good morning," she said, walking into the boardroom. "I'm Evelyn Springdale, the mayor's representative. I'm looking forward to meeting all of you."

The buzz in the room cut off abruptly, and Leann stood up. "Where's the mayor?" She gestured to a pile of placards leaning against the wall in the corner. "We were going to picket peacefully out front and he invited us inside. We've been sitting here for over an hour."

Taking a few steps toward the signs, Evie saw slogans like, "Back off Breeders," "Pick your Battles," and "Breeders Know Best." Evidently, rumors about the new regulations had leaked; they just hadn't leaked as far as Evie's own ears. How was she going to stickhandle angry stakeholders when she didn't even know the issues?

The only available seat was on the far side of the table, so she made her way around. "Coffee's on the way," she said.

"And the mayor?" Leann persisted. "We don't want some slick PR person feeding us bullsh—"

"Leann, come on," someone said. "Let's get started on the right foot."

The voice belonged to a beautiful blonde woman who looked familiar. Evie was still trying to place her when she tripped over something—a work boot, perhaps—and stumbled right into the blonde woman's lap.

"I am so sorry," she said, trying to extricate herself without putting her hands anywhere they shouldn't go. Finally, she got one hand on the wooden arm of the chair and another on the table and pushed up. There were snickers all around, particularly among those sitting closest to Leann.

"Wow, that coffee cannot come soon enough," Evie said, slipping into the empty seat. Giving the blonde woman a sheepish smile, she added, "I hope you'll forgive the rude introduction."

"We met the other night anyway," the woman said. "At the hospital fundraiser. I'm Arianna Torrance, a dog breeder."

"If you call those puffball designer hybrids dogs," Leann muttered.

"I do, actually." Ari smiled at Leann. "And I'm just as concerned about these new regulations as any other breeder. I know most of you are beagle people but several of us represent other breeds."

"Or non-breeds."

There was a snicker around the table, and Evie decided to intervene. Ari was Remi's friend, and she didn't want to see her bullied. "I'm sure the mayor would agree that all breeds are equal in Dorset Hills. So let's hear what's really bothering you today."

Leann's mouth dropped open. "What's bothering us? How about breeder restrictions? How about site visits and jumping through hoops for certification? Isn't that enough to picket over, PR lady?"

Evie pressed her lips together, wishing the coffee would arrive and defuse the tension. She hoped Chloe had the sense to order some muffins to sweeten everyone up.

Ari caught Evie's eye and then stood. "I'm glad we didn't have to picket today. It's great that we get to sit in this boardroom and express our concerns about the pending breeder regulations. We all knew these would come at some point, and we probably all agree that something was needed to control unscrupulous breeders from profiting at the expense of the dogs."

"Puppy mills," several people hissed.

"They can crack down on unethical operations without making honest breeders turn handsprings," Leann said. "I've been producing prizewinning beagles for 15 years, and now dog cops will be crawling all over my property and telling me how to do my job."

"We don't know what's in the regulations yet," Ari said.

"I know what I heard," Leann said. "And it sounded like I'll only be able to have six breeding dogs at one time. That's going to seriously affect my business."

"Mine, too," Ari said, looking at Evie. "If it's true."

"I can't comment yet," Evie said. "The policymakers haven't shared their proposal."

Leann threw something on the table hard enough to dent the wood. It skittered across the table and spun in a circle before coming to rest. It was a car key, and someone sent it sailing back.

"What good are you, PR lady?" Leann asked. "They didn't even bother to tell you what they're leaking."

Evie took a deep breath and centered herself. She felt blindsided, but she could fall back on the time-honored rules of stakeholder engagement. Listen. Engage. Respect opinions. Offer hope.

"If that's what you've heard, I understand why you'd be concerned," she said. "But if government staff like me haven't yet seen the regulations, it's safe to say they're not etched in stone. Why don't we talk through what's important to you, and I'll take the information back to the mayor."

"Like he'd listen to you."

"Like he'd listen to anyone," someone else shouted.

"We'll have to give up our dogs," Leann said. "Don't you realize that? These aren't ordinary pets to us. We've invested a lot in our breeding stock and we'd go to extremes to protect them. Tell the mayor *that*."

Leann raised her palm and slapped it down on the table. Others followed suit. Slap-slap-slap-slap. The palms closed into fists and the slaps turned to thumping.

Finally, Evie got to her feet. "Quiet. Or I'm leaving. And since the mayor is off site, you'll lose this chance to share what you want the City to know about your work."

Leann's mouth opened but Ari's voice rang out first. "Let's use this opportunity to get on the record," she said.

"Seconded." The woman who spoke had introduced herself earlier as Ruth Banks. Now she turned to Leann. "I'd like to be heard. How about you, dear?" Maybe it was Ruth's gray hair and motherly demeanor, but something settled Leann down.

Over the next hour, Evie let each person speak, inquiring about their breed of choice and the size of their operation.

"Question," Evie said, circling the table with a pot of hot coffee. "And please, no one trip me this time." There was a sheepish snicker that confirmed her suspicion. "If the new regulations are meant to crack down on unethical back-yard breeders, how can we help the City accomplish that without affecting quality breeders like yourselves?"

"Hire more dog cops to investigate suspicious leads, rather than pester decent breeders," Leann said. "Duh."

Evie stopped with the coffee pot dangling over Leann's shoulder just long enough to make her squirm. "Would there be interest in forming a committee to brainstorm ideas?"

"Forget it," Leann said. "We're not on your side, in case you didn't notice."

Ari raised her hand. "I'm in. I'll write a submission stating our concerns."

Evie sat down again. "I'll place it on his desk personally."

Downing her coffee with a quick flick of the wrist, Leann stood up. "We'll try your way first, Arianna. And then when that doesn't work—and it won't—we'll try mine."

She tossed the paper cup onto the table and turned. Another flick of her wrist and the rest of the breeders followed. Even Ari fell into line. When she reached the door, she turned back and mouthed "sorry."

Evie nodded and shrugged to convey "you're just doing your job and I'm doing mine."

But handling tech titans in California had never felt quite as intimidating as a room full of irate dog breeders.

"HEY," Zeke said, meeting her in the reception area as she came back into the office after lunch. "I've been looking for you."

"Sorry," she said, hanging up her coat. "The place I rented is a wreck. I needed to meet with a contractor."

Technically, it was her second lunch break as she'd driven home twice to feed the baby capybara and make sure the cat was doing his job. She'd found them curled up together in the bathtub. It was the kind of scene that would go viral on social media. Too bad she could never post it.

"Everything okay, Red?" he asked. "You look tired. Nick will have my head if we don't treat his sister right."

Running a hand over her now-frizzy hair, she forced a

smile. She preferred to stay hermetically sealed on work days, but her personal pet crisis prevented that. "I'm fine, thanks. But I don't like the nickname."

"Nick said you loved it! He specifically asked me to call you that."

"Why doesn't that surprise me?"

Zeke gave her a blazing smile, well pleased. "Glad you're not upset about the beagle reps. I heard it got heated."

Chloe the tattletale slipped one earbud out to enjoy the discussion.

"Except for the chip in the table, it went as well as it could, really. I sent you my notes. Are they right about the new regulations?"

"Mostly," he said, shrugging. "There's no way to keep everyone happy. You know that."

"Can't you at least grandfather existing breeders? A lot of them moved here and invested heavily to set up just because of the Dog Town brand. They stand to lose a lot from restricting the number of dogs. Tens of thousands in some cases."

"The mayor doesn't do policy by committee," Zeke said. "He does what's best for the city as a whole. And a regulated breeding sector is best for all."

"But it makes sense to listen to the people most affected, especially when they're mobilized."

"We'll drown them out with the puppy mill message," he said. "All we have to do is zap a few shady operations and get plenty of good coverage."

"Zapping puppy mills is great, but it wouldn't hurt to listen to reputable breeders, would it? I recommend forming a committee to get input."

Zeke shrugged again and his smile turned indulgent.

"All right. If you feel that strongly about it, I'll leave it in your capable hands. I thought you'd be busy enough getting the Easter festival organized."

Chloe put her earbud back in, a smirk playing on her burgundy-tinted lips. Evie suspected Chloe's job had become infinitely more interesting since she'd joined the staff.

"The rottweiler reps are calling," she said. "And the French bulldog people are on hold. Which do you want first?"

Evie didn't even turn as she headed for her office. "Surprise me."

CHAPTER TEN

"Ready?" she asked, zipping a pale blue hoodie over a pair of jeans. She wanted to look casual. Ordinary. Everywoman. One glance in the bathroom mirror shot that hope to hell. Both of her parents had lovely dark hair, but the sneaky recessive red gene had struck both Nick and herself. It meant she would never ever blend in with the crowd—not until she was 80, anyway. Twisting her hair into a knot, she slipped a gray baseball cap over it. "Best I can do," she told Roberto. "Stay out of sight, okay? I'm hard to miss at the best of times. With you, it's impossible."

He jumped out of the bathtub, where the little capybara had fallen asleep after an hour of wandering around the tub and nibbling the lettuce and guinea pig food she'd picked up after work, at the suggestion of Google. It surprised her that a days-old baby was already showing interest in adult food as well as formula. What surprised her more was the range of vocalization this little lady had. She whistled and grunted and chirped and chirred. Mostly she squealed, a high-pitched sound that felt like a drill to the eardrum.

"We only have an hour or two tops before she wakes up

and freaks out that you're gone," she said. "You've done such a good job as nanny that she's imprinted on you."

He wove his signature figure eight around her feet and purred, clearly quite taken with himself.

"We have to get her home, though," Evie said, stepping out of his loops and heading for the door. "Or at least reunited with her family. Before you get too attached."

He protested with little mews all the way through the kitchen.

"If you could kindly lead me directly back to where you found her last night, we could get this resolved, no fuss no muss. Understood?"

Staring up at her, he blinked a few times in silence.

"I said...*understood*?"

He gave a drawn-out meow.

"Good. Let's get on it. Stay in the shadows and do your best to lead me on a path fit for humans. I can't go crawling through neighbors' yards or climbing fences. You know how clumsy I am, and subtle is the name of this game."

She stopped with her hand on the door. "As if talking to a cat like it understands me is subtle. People would talk about that more than my climbing into their yard." She opened the door and let Roberto pass in front of her. "No chit-chat after this. Let's act normal."

Up until a week ago, she'd been exceedingly normal, rare hair gene aside. Now this pet-phobe was skulking around her new neighborhood with a precocious cat, while their giant guinea pig baby napped. She'd expected life to be different in Dog Town but not *this* different.

Roberto trotted along the hedges in the shadows, far enough ahead that they wouldn't be seen together, but not so far that she couldn't spot him in the fading light. She'd hoped to get out earlier, but Letitia, the capybara, wouldn't go down for her nap. Now they only had a half hour before sundown. But it should be enough to find where he'd visited last night. Roberto was capable of covering several blocks on his own; his trip to Nick's house had proven that. Doing it while carrying a 1.5 lb load was another story, however. He couldn't have come far, and she assumed he wanted her to know where he'd found it.

They circled her block quickly. Roberto lagged behind on the back half, as if to let her know she was on the wrong path.

"Careful," she said, as they moved on. It unnerved her to cross at the light with him, but he raced across ahead of her like a pro and sat down beside a tree to wait for her to catch up.

The next block seemed like a better option. The houses were bigger and nicer, and had a lot more property. Most lawns featured at least one twig art dog. A local artisan was making a killing on these. Apparently they were breed specific, but they all looked pretty much the same to Evie.

Roberto zigzagged from bush to shrub to tree, staying out of the way. Finally, at the second to last house, he ran right up to the door and sat on the porch.

"Is this it?" she whispered. "It can't be. The house is too small. If the mama capybara is as chatty as Letitia, all the neighbors would know."

She didn't have much choice but to try knocking. Roberto had parked himself beside a planter and wasn't moving.

"This is a bad idea," she muttered, dropping a knocker shaped like a poodle.

There were footsteps on the other side, and then the door opened. A woman with shoulder-length dark hair offered a smile. "Evelyn, right?" she said. "We met at the hospital fundraiser. I'm Mim Gardiner. Remi's friend."

"Yes, of course. Hello." Her throat clenched because she was unsure of what to say next. "I hope I'm not intruding."

"Are you going door to door for the City?" Mim asked.

"Actually, yes," Evie said. "Just an informal poll to see how regular citizens feel about potential new regulations for dog breeders."

Mim opened the door wider. "Come in. I'll make a pot of decaf and tell you what I really think about this political regime."

Uh-oh. That could take awhile and she really couldn't be away long. But Roberto clearly had a plan, because he waltzed inside ahead of her.

"Oh, wait," Mim said. "You probably shouldn't bring your cat inside. I have a—"

A red streak came down the hall and pounced. The mid-sized dog had planned to take Roberto down like a gazelle on the Serengeti. Instead, Roberto jumped onto the hall table and the dog smashed into its legs. The table tipped, dumping a heavy glass bowl to the floor with a thud. Amazingly, it didn't break, but there was a clatter as keys fell out. The cat jumped from the table to the banister and balanced there, tail swishing, as the dog leaped at him, barking.

"George, stop," Mim said. George continued to jump, and Roberto reached down to swat at him.

"Leave it. *Down*."

The voice was so commanding that Evie's legs almost folded into a "down." George's did and he turned toward the kitchen doorway, where Cori Hogan stood with her thumbs hooked into the pockets of her jeans. She wasn't wearing her gloves with the orange flipping fingers.

"Oh. It's you," Cori said.

She might as well spit and be done with it, Evie thought. "Yep. It's me."

"She's canvassing door to door to get our take on the new regulations for dog breeders," Mim said.

"*Proposed* new regs," Evie said. "We just began public consultations today."

Mim brushed past Cori, who didn't move out of the way till the last minute. She looked up at Evie with contempt, and Evie was seriously tempted to mirror that expression.

"You're canvassing with a cat?" Cori said, watching as Roberto leapt lightly over George's prone body and followed Mim into the kitchen. "That's risky in Dog Town. I heard the mayor wants to regulate outdoor cats, as well."

"He's a stray," Evie said, sliding onto a stool at the counter. "He's been following me everywhere. It's embarrassing, really, but I can't shake him."

Roberto jumped into her lap and clung there, digging in his claws until she yipped.

"Match made in heaven," Cori said, snickering. "Why can't the City let owners decide whether to let their cats outside?"

"Well, we're not consulting on cat regulations at this point." Evie stood to shake off Roberto, and he dropped to the floor with an indignant mew. "It's dog breeders we're concerned about."

"The City should leave breeders alone," Mim said, sliding a mug under the spout of her single shot coffee machine. "My best friend, Arianna Torrance, is a caring, committed breeder who runs a legitimate operation. She wants to expand and why shouldn't she, when there's a waiting list for her puppies?"

"Just to play devil's advocate..." Cori began.

"Cori, you're here to train George," Mim said. "When Evie comes to your door, you can play devil's advocate."

"She won't come to my door, because I moved out of Dorset Hills after Bill Bradshaw got elected. I took my tax dollars away in silent protest."

"Silent? Since when?" Mim passed a mug of coffee to Evie, along with a carton of cream and a sugar bowl.

"Good point. I can say what I want," Cori said, accepting the next cup of coffee. She watched Evie add cream and sugar and then made a show of drinking her coffee scorching and black. "And what I want to say is that for every reputable breeder like Ari, there are two others who aren't. Two others who crowd their dogs, breed them back to the same line, breed them too young, breed them too often, and just generally, breed unhealthy dogs in inappropriate conditions."

Evie's eyes widened. "You know this how?"

Taking another sip, Cori asked, "Do you really want to know how I know?"

"Ah. Rescue Mafia activity."

"We've visited quite a few breeders in recent years to give their dogs a better life."

"In other words, raided them," Evie said.

"No comment. Other than to offer the opinion that oversight of breeders isn't a bad thing, as long as it's to benefit the dogs, and not the deep pockets of the City."

"Interesting," Evie said. "I actually value your opinion, Cori."

Cori smirked over the rim of her cup. "You say that with some surprise."

Evie shrugged. "Maybe I got the wrong impression of you."

"No, you got the impression I wanted you to have. But

people don't always fall into the neat categories you set out for us."

"You don't know me that well," Evie said.

Cori looked at the cat sitting at Evie's feet. "True. I wouldn't have taken you for a cat lady. I thought I smelled a pet-hater when we met."

A snort almost sent coffee up Evie's nose. "You're not so far wrong. But this guy is growing on me."

Still staring at Roberto, Cori said, "No offense, but—"

Evie raised her free hand. "What comes after that lead-in is always offensive."

Cori grinned before continuing. "I wanted to hate you for being the mayor's lackey, but now I can't. Wandering around with this cat makes you unhateable. In fact, it makes you interesting. But now I'm worried for you."

Evie scooped up the cat and he collapsed on his back in her arms, kneading the air. "Why is that?"

"Because interesting people—and good people—don't last long working for this regime. We lost Marti Forrester a few months back. The mayor broke her."

"The mayor won't break Evelyn," Mim said. "She's trained in political machinations."

"She's rocking that cat like an infant," Cori said. "It's as bad as Remi and her beagle-baby. Something like this could cost you a job in Dog Town. It doesn't take much. Just a whiff of personality."

Setting the cat down again, Evie rested her chin on one hand and tapped the counter with the fingers of the other. "I'll be okay, Cori, but thanks for your concern."

Cori stood on the other side of the island and mirrored Evie's pose, right down to the tapping fingers. "One day you're going to need my help, Evelyn. And, you know what?"

"I'm sure you'll tell me," Evie said, suddenly weary.

"When that day comes, I'll help you. Because if you'll let this stray cat wrap you around his paw, you deserve to be helped."

Evie stared down at the counter. Her eyes stung with tears, and she didn't want Cori and Mim to see them. It was time to go. She'd made a mistake in trusting Roberto to bring her where she needed to be. Yet he seemed well pleased with himself, if purring was any indication. Obviously she was giving him too much credit. He was just a cat, after all.

"You've got me all wrong," she said, getting up from the stool and heading out of the kitchen.

Cori followed her, finally releasing George from his down-stay. The cat brushed right past him and George shrunk backwards.

"I'm never wrong," Cori said.

"Never?" Mim asked.

"Rarely," Cori corrected. "Anyway, I'm not wrong about Evelyn. There's more to her than meets the eye. This cat isn't just a stray. He's a familiar."

"A what?" Evie asked, over her shoulder.

"Look it up," Cori said. "And remember, I didn't say you're a witch."

Evie stopped with her hand on the doorknob. "I've been called worse."

"Me too," Cori said, grinning.

"True," Mim said. "Much worse."

"Why doesn't that surprise me?" Evie opened the door and Roberto flitted outside.

"Because you're a witch?" Cori was right on her heels. "Crystal ball and all that?"

"Oh man, I'd love one of those," Evie said. "Probably wouldn't have been fired so often."

Cori tipped her head to one side, looking like a little brown bird. A wren perhaps, instead of the crow Evie saw the other day. "How often, exactly?" she asked.

Evie rolled her eyes. "I don't need a crystal ball to know better than to answer that."

"No need," Cori said. "Eight's my lucky number."

"Impressive. You have good sources." Now she sounded even more weary. She usually carried her past easily, but not tonight.

"Dog rescue relies on a network of confidential contacts," Cori said. "People underestimate us and that works in our favor."

Sticking out her hand, Evie said, "I will never underestimate you again."

Cori started raising her hand, thought better of it, and let it drop. "Sorry. You're on the mayor's team, and I'm no faker."

Evie nodded. "Understood. I trade in fake."

"Nah. What you have here..." Cori's finger traced an invisible line between Evie and Roberto. "That can't be faked. That's how I know."

"Know what?"

Cori stepped back and started to close the door. "Know it's just a matter of time before Dog Town chews you up and spits you out."

"Cori, that's mean even for you," Mim said, pulling the door open. She pressed a slip of paper into Evie's hand and gave her a knowing nod.

"It's not mean if it's true," Cori said.

"Since when?" Mim asked, hauling her back inside. "Good luck, Evie."

"Nine's her lucky number," Cori said, as the door closed.

CHAPTER ELEVEN

The car wasn't what Evie expected. She'd been thinking government-issue black sedan, like the one the mayor piloted around town. But someone waved to her from a gray Prius. She walked across the small parking lot outside the drugstore and met the driver smile for smile.

"I'm Kinney Butterfield," said the woman behind the wheel. "Jump in."

Evie went around the car and got into the passenger seat before offering her hand. "Evelyn Springdale. Thank you for meeting me."

"Don't thank me," Kinney said. "I'm happy to help any friend of Mim's. Besides, it's my job." She turned the key in the ignition. "Sort of."

"You're a canine corrections officer, not a tour guide," Evie said.

"Dog cop," Kinney said, her smile contorting a little. "At least, that's what everyone calls us." She paused at the exit of the parking lot. "Where to?"

"Just show me around town. Talk to me about your work, and the problems you see. Off the record, of course."

"Nothing's really off the record, is it? We both know better."

"You have my word," Evie said. "That may not count for much."

Kinney gave her a sideways glance. "It does. Cori Hogan likes you."

"She does?" That surprised her. And it surprised her more that she even cared about Cori's opinion.

"We don't agree on everything," Kinney said, flicking dark hair out of her eyes. "But Cori knows a good dog person when she meets one, and I do, too."

"But I'm not a dog person," Evie said, and then covered her mouth with her hand. "That's a terrible thing to say. I like some dogs well enough. I just... have allergies."

Shaking her head, Kinney turned left, away from City Hall and the heaviest population of bronze statues. "You are a dog person. You just don't know it yet."

"I think I would know if—"

Kinney lifted her hand off the wheel and waved dismissively. "One day it will spring to life. You just need to meet the right dog."

"And Cori said *I'm* the witch."

Kinney's laugh was warm and infectious. "She's such a sweetheart."

"I have an idea where we could go," Evie said.

"I figured you would. Which Lab do I take?"

It took Evie a second to realize she meant which Labrador retriever statue. There were five bronze sentinels at points around the periphery of the city proper. To her, they all looked the same, but to longer-term residents, there were subtle differences. "I want to visit Arianna Torrance," she said. "The dog breeder."

"I know Ari," Kinney said, making a left. "Goldendoodle hybrids. Beautiful dogs, though I prefer a purebred golden retriever. Like your brother's."

Evie turned to stare at the side of Kinney's head. "You know my brother?"

"Nope, but I've admired his golden. Perfect conformation. It's my breed of choice."

"Where did you see Clive?"

"Around. They go pretty much everywhere together, right? I assume he took the dog with him to North Carolina."

Clearing her throat, Evie said, "Were you asked to do a background check on me?"

"Nope," Kinney said. After a pause, she added, "I don't wait to be asked. I like to know things."

Rifling through her bag for lip gloss, Evie muttered, "I'm not that interesting."

"Seriously? If I read about your life in a book I'd think it was made up. I mean, you've been fired—"

"I know. It's not as bad as it sounds."

"If you ask me, you were framed at least half of those times, maybe more." She pressed the pedal down as they passed a Lab statue and entered the suburbs. "And the accidents. I mean, what are the chances?"

"You know about—?" She cut off the words and pressed her lips together.

"I know you've been in hospital ERs eight times in as many years. Concussions, a broken arm, cracked ribs, couple of bad sprains. If you'd had just one boyfriend, I'd be wondering about him."

Evie's eyes narrowed. "My mom always said I was accident prone."

"Getting hit by a car twice? It'd be easier to win the lottery."

A shiver ran down Evie's spine and she buttoned her jacket to her chin. "Sometimes it feels like the potholes of life are waiting to swallow me up." She turned the heating vents toward her. "Can we talk about something else now? Like pending regulations that have dog breeders up in arms?"

"Ah. Well, I don't always agree with how the City tackles these things, but I believe there needs to be more control. We've had to disband six operations in the past couple of months. The conditions were deplorable."

"I'm sorry to hear that. And a bit surprised, because it's Dog Town. I thought everyone adored dogs... especially breeders."

"It's like everywhere else on the planet. There are good people, bad people and a whole lot in between. Some breeders honestly believe dogs are just animals and like living in outdoor kennels. Others sleep with eight dogs on a king-sized bed. Who's right?"

"Keeping dogs in anything less than five-star accommodation goes against Dog Town branding."

Kinney nodded. "The problem with regulations—or at least the ones I've seen—is that there's no gray area. It's 'my way or the highway.'"

"The highway might be the better option. Land is cheaper in Pemsville or Brenton. From what I hear, they're more relaxed about... well, everything."

"That's why there are even more puppy mills outside of Dorset Hills. Greedy people selling what oblivious people are buying. They won't always wait for a pup from a quality breeder, and they don't do their due diligence."

Turning left onto a long, quiet street with large, beautiful homes, Kinney said, "Some of our good breeders would fare better elsewhere, but they don't want to be forced out by politics. Can't blame them, either."

"It's a curse to be able to see both sides, isn't it?" Evie asked, grinning.

"Sometimes." Kinney nodded as she pulled into a driveway. "It makes my job harder. Black and white is easier in law enforcement."

The house wasn't exactly shabby, but it didn't have the curb appeal of others on the street. Where some neighbors already had urns of hardy spring flowers, and flowering trees throwing up colorful arms to the cool breeze, Ari's house was stark. It suggested an owner who had more on her mind than home decor.

Even before they opened the car doors, the din of barking reached them. There had to be at least 10 dogs inside. Evie steeled herself to be swarmed by slobbering, smelly beasts. So many dogs together could never be civil.

The front door opened and the barking subsided. Ari stood framed in the doorway, with smooth blonde hair, flawless makeup, nice black pants and what appeared to be a black cashmere sweater. What dog breeder dressed that way at home? It was almost as if she knew they were coming.

"Welcome," she said. "I put some coffee on for you."

"I didn't see you text her," Evie whispered to Kinney as they walked up the stairs.

"We've already established that you miss a lot of things," Kinney whispered back. "Like potholes."

"Thank you for seeing us, Ari," Evie said, offering her hand.

Ari shook her hand and then stood back to let her pass. Across the hall sat a long row of dogs in colors ranging from cream to deep red. All butts were planted, but there was wriggling and swishing of tails, and a couple of them whined in excitement. Evie worried they'd explode when Ari released them.

"I know you're not a dog person, Evie," Ari said, taking their coats. "Do you want me to put them outside?"

"She's a dog person," Kinney said. "She just doesn't know it yet."

"Ah. Well, mine will reveal all," Ari said. "No one can resist them."

"Let them stay in," Evie said. "I'm here to see a typical breeder's operation."

"There's no such thing as typical," Ari said, gesturing for them to precede her into the kitchen. Once they were inside, she clapped to release the dogs. They surged in around the guests, but there was no jumping. Several licked Evie's hands and she crossed them over her chest.

Taking a seat at the sleek oak table, Evie stared down at the muzzles lining up on her thigh, one after the other. There was only room for six, and the rest jockeyed for position. Ari didn't call them off. Instead she smiled as she poured coffee into three mugs.

"You're cute, I'll give you that," Evie told the dogs. "And no sneezing. Yet."

Sliding a mug in front of her, Ari pointed to a golden retriever. "She's my only shedder. The rest are hypoallergenic."

"So that's how you get away with wearing black."

"Exactly," Ari said, offering cream and sugar. "It's important to look nice, even for dog breeders."

"Not everyone at that City Hall meeting agreed with you," Evie said. "Leann Cosgrove for example."

Ari sighed as she perched across from them. "Leann and I butt heads a lot, but we both love our dogs. She's old school. Her hounds live outside in kennels and their only training is on field trials. I raise companion dogs, and I treat them like kids. At least by breeder standards."

"They're well behaved," Evie said, gingerly patting one between the ears. The others immediately pressed in to get attention. The one at the end of the row kept its nose on her knee, staring at her with sweet eyes while its fringed tail wagged. "You're such a lady."

"Gentleman, actually. That's Thurston Howl. I was intending to breed him but I'm afraid he's too soft."

Evie reached over and stroked his fur. "Seems just soft enough to me."

Ari laughed. "I mean his temperament. He's very gentle, almost to the point of skittishness. I prefer my breeding dogs to be rock solid." She gestured to the larger red dog sitting at her side. "You could drive a truck through the front window and this one wouldn't flinch. Thurston would hide under the bed."

"Aw, Thurston, I feel for you, buddy," Evie said. "He's a beautiful color, and his eyes have soul."

Kinney raised her hand to her ear. "I hear something... Ah. It's the sound of a hard heart cracking open."

"Funny," Evie said. "Almost as funny as Cori Hogan, but not quite."

Kinney rolled her eyes. "Touché."

Sipping her coffee, Ari watched Evie over the rim. "So, why are you really here, Evie?"

"To ask for help. Obviously that first meeting didn't go well, and I can admit when I don't understand the landscape. The mayor brought me on board to prevent PR issues, and I feel this could boil over without careful handling."

Ari nodded. "You didn't hear it from me, but some of

the more militant breeders are organizing to protest. It's not my way, but I've been on the wrong side of breeders before and it was awful."

The dogs had mostly drifted away, but Thurston was still there. "What happened? With the breeders, I mean?"

"I used to breed goldens and even show them. When I switched to hybrids, it got the purebred community up in arms. The more successful I got, the more they disparaged my practices. They ganged up online, in particular, and those comments live forever."

"Trolling?"

Ari nodded. "Like mean girls in the schoolyard. Only anonymous. And global."

Thurston had gradually inched up so she could scratch his wiggly bum. "What did you do about it?"

"Mostly I let positive word of mouth combat the negative. But I also did something I advise you to do: made the right friends. Leann for starters. She has a lot of influence. Ruth Banks is another. Interesting lady. She used to be a zookeeper, and has stories to tell."

Keeping one hand on Thurston, Evie typed notes into her phone with the other. "What will appease them?"

"Allow outdoor kennels. Keep the number of dogs on the premises as high as you can." Ari looked at Kinney. "Focus investigation on health and safety issues. Honestly, while we don't agree, most breeders in Dorset Hills care about their dogs. Even too much."

Evie sighed. "I'll do what I can. I'm pushing for a delay to allow consultation."

"I'll pass along any information I can," Ari said.

Kinney finally spoke. "Don't jeopardize your standing in the community, Ari. I'll probably hear what you hear. I've got a few sources."

"Let's hope it all blows over in time for Easter," Ari said. "I'm looking forward to the festival." She watched as Thurston offered a stuffed animal to Evie. "You can borrow Thurston for the treasure hunt if you want."

Evie felt a flutter of excitement at the thought, but tamped it down. "I'll be too busy to participate myself, unfortunately. But I hope to meet this sweetheart again."

Kinney tapped her watch. "We've got to go. But Ari, you'd better give Evie first dibs on Thurston if you let him go."

"Oh, stop it," Evie said, as they left. "I'm not a dog person and never will be."

Hopping into the car, Kinney said, "I guess you've got your hands full already."

"I do, actually. This job is more than I bargained for."

"And then there's your houseguest. You seem to gravitate to ginger."

Evie turned to stare at her. "Pardon me?"

"Ginger cats are the most gregarious, you know. I read it in National Geographic."

"It's just a stray I'm helping out for a couple of weeks. You *are* spying on me."

"Not at all," Kinney said. "As I said, I like to know things. I store them away in case I need them down the road."

"Well, I'd prefer it if you'd lock that one up tight. The mayor doesn't like cats, and didn't want to hire me when he thought I did."

"Of course," Kinney said. "It's great what you're doing. But keep him safe, okay? There's some crazy stuff going on lately."

"Like what, exactly? Anything the mayor should know about?"

Kinney shook her head and sealed her lips for the rest of the drive. Before long, she pulled the car up in front of Evie's house, without asking for directions.

Thanking her, Evie got out of the car. "Keep me posted on the crazy stuff, okay? So it doesn't bite me in the butt."

"Think about taking Thurston," Kinney said. "It would be good protection. And say hi to Roberto for me."

CHAPTER TWELVE

The scream hurt Evie's throat as it ripped out, and it startled the cat. He dropped his prey and she screamed again as it shot under the sofa.

Make that slithered.

The snake was about four feet long and bright yellow. She'd never seen anything like it—had never wanted to see anything like it. She was mildly phobic of most creatures. But snakes? That was full-on.

"Get it out of here," she yelled. "Now!"

Roberto stared at her, green eyes fixed and unblinking. He looked disappointed, but that had to be her own projection. Cats didn't look disappointed. They weren't capable of emotions like that.

"Roberto, please." If commands didn't work, maybe pleading would. "I don't know if that thing is poisonous. But I can tell you that my brother will kill us both when he finds it... if the snake hasn't killed us first."

After Kinney had showed so much interest in Roberto the day before, she'd decided it would be safer to keep the animals at Nick's. Kinney seemed trustworthy but she was awfully curious. Besides, Nick's house was in perfect condition and Roberto would be less likely to escape.

Only obviously he had done just that. She'd come to Nick's after work, and with her hands full of groceries and pet supplies, he'd shot right through her feet and disappeared.

She'd passed the time sitting beside the bathtub that contained Letitia. The pup had taken more formula, nibbled on guinea pig food and fresh produce, and splashed in her dish tub of water. She made chirring sounds that seemed contented enough, and had plenty of energy. But eventually, she began bleating inconsolably—something she never did when her cat nanny was around. After an hour, Evie started worrying he wouldn't come back at all. Then what would she do? Finally there was a scratch at the door to let her know he'd returned from his jaunt.

Dusk had fallen, but the yellow snake was hard to miss.

"Get it," she said now. "I don't care where it came from. I am not touching that thing."

Roberto scraped at her brother's carpet with one paw, as if to say that he found her no better than excrement in his litter box. Then he stalked past her and went into the bathroom. The incessant bleating cut off abruptly with the cat-nanny at his post.

"Get back here," she called after him. "What am I supposed to do?"

In the silence that followed, she pondered. If she left the room to get a box and gloves, the snake might slither off, and she'd have no idea where it ended up. There was no way her nerves could handle hours of poking around under furniture looking for it. No, she'd stay put until help arrived.

Pulling out her phone, she muttered a quick prayer that

he'd pick up and almost wept when he did. "Jon, can you come, please? To my brother's."

"Is it the capy? Or Roberto?"

"Neither. The cat brought home something else."

"Another capy?"

"Worse. It's a snake, and it's under the couch. I'm afraid to move in case it hightails it somewhere else and I never find it."

"Technically snakes don't have tails."

"*Please.*"

She hated playing the damsel in distress. Normally she was more than capable of solving the problems life threw in her path, even when life also threw *her* in the path. But snakes were something else. Surely Jon wouldn't blame her for panicking.

"Evie, I still have patients. It'll be an hour before I can get away. Are you sure you can't handle this?"

She tried to push down her panic and then whispered, "I guess so. If I have to."

"Or you can call animal control. That's the better option, of course."

She shook her head, forgetting he couldn't hear it.

"Evie?"

"I'll handle it," she said. "Do they have ears?"

"They feel vibration with their tongues. So you'll want to move calmly and slowly. And wear gloves, of course. In case—"

"—it's poisonous?"

"Most aren't." His voice was soothing. "Send me a photo and I'll confirm it."

She mouthed another silent prayer.

"Evie?" he said again, when she didn't answer. "Just turn on the flash and stick your phone under the couch. Take a quick pic and I'll tell you the next steps."

Swallowing hard, she crouched beside the couch. No way was she getting on her hands and knees. The thing would swarm her and she would pass out from terror. At least if she were unconscious she wouldn't feel the toxins seeping through her.

"Is it a quick death?" she asked, gingerly lifting the skirt on the couch. Bending over, her hair dusted the floor as she directed the phone into the darkness.

"Just get a picture," he said.

The snake was coiled tight. "It's not moving. What if Roberto killed it?"

"If he's protecting the capy, he probably didn't kill the snake. He's a collector, not a killer. So... photo?"

She took the photo, dropped the skirt and backed to the middle of the room. Her hand was shaking so hard she could barely press send.

"Still there?" Jon asked.

"Snakes and snails and puppy dog tails," she said. "That's what boys are made of."

"This one sure is," he said, and then, "Oh."

"It's poisonous, isn't it?"

"Actually no. It's a Burmese python—an albino. Rare and prized for its striking color."

"Yeah, it's a beaut."

"This one's just a youth, but they can grow to be..." He cleared his throat. "Quite large, actually. Look, I'll cancel my last appointments and come over."

Relief mixed with resentment. "You're only coming because it's rare and striking. A collector's item."

There was a shuffle at the other end as he gathered his things. "Honestly? If it were venomous or an adult python, I would have called animal control whether you liked it or not. And they'd have carted away the cat and the capy, too."

She backed to the closest chair, collapsed and drew up her feet. "I'm sorry, Jon. I'm just…"

"Terrified. I know. Now hang tight and I'll be there in half an hour."

More strangled sounds came out of her mouth and then, "That long?"

"Never mind," he said. "I'll teleport and be there in five. Deep breaths, okay?"

"YOU'RE SURE?"

"Very sure. I've secured the terrarium with bricks."

"You didn't have something with a lock?"

"It'll be fine. Roberto is on security detail."

The cat had emerged from the bathroom the second Jon had walked in the door. He oversaw the extraction of the snake and was now perched atop the glass terrarium Jon had brought from the veterinary clinic. Evie was lying on the couch. She'd gotten light-headed when Jon scooped up the writhing snake on a broom handle, and when he grasped it in his bare hand, the room actually spun. The sandwich she'd eaten six hours earlier was threatening to make a reappearance.

"Why is Roberto doing this?" she asked, fighting tears.

"I'm just a vet," he said, grinning. "I can tell you how his body works, not his brain."

"He clearly doesn't have one. If he had any gratitude at all for our saving him, he wouldn't bring things home that could kill us."

Roberto's tail swished faster, as if he understood what

they were saying. He couldn't, of course. She was semi-delusional from fright.

"You're exaggerating. Letitia is only capable of killing lettuce. And the snake isn't a threat either, unless you're a mouse."

She opened her eyes and stared up at him. "I am a mouse."

"You're plenty brave," he said, smiling. "It takes courage to offer advice to the mayor. Let alone challenge unhappy dog breeders. One snake is not going to get you down."

"Newsflash: I'm down."

"Not for long. I'm going to get you a glass of water."

She called after him. "You'll find it in the cupboard beside the fridge in a bottle marked 'bourbon.'"

He laughed. "I'm glad you're recovering your sense of humor. You're going to need it."

By the time he got back with two fingers of bourbon in a juice glass for each of them, she was sitting up. "You've got to take it away, Jon. There is no way I am feeding mice to a snake. For starters, I'd have to lift the lid and that will never happen. It'll die under my watch, and I won't grieve."

He perched on the other end of the couch. "I'll take it. Only because I won't be responsible for your heart failing. But realize it does drag me even deeper into this situation, when I'd rather involve the City."

"If you really wanted to involve the City, I expect you would have," she said. "You don't trust them to fix this properly either."

He stared at his hands. "Maybe you're right. I'd like to be able to trust them... but I don't, really. Still, I feel out of my depth. I'm more convinced than ever that there's an exotic pet ring. The albino Burmese python is very much in demand due to its lovely shade. This one has brothers and sisters."

She closed her eyes and shuddered. "Don't even. I wish Buttercup no harm—now that I know you're taking her. And I'm even more committed to solving this puzzle."

When she opened her eyes, Roberto was picking his way up the couch toward her. He stepped into her lap, turned twice, and curled up. Then he unleashed a purr that practically shook the room. When she didn't offer her hand, he pushed his head under her fingers and angled it so she could stroke his chin.

"Seems like you two are thicker than thieves," Jon said, smiling. He'd brought Gilda inside after the snake was contained and now she settled at his feet, as if this was all in a day's work.

Evie stared at the cat in her lap. "He's never done this before. I guess he's getting tired of playing nanny to a big gerbil and wants human contact."

Roberto flexed his claws into her leg and she gave a bleat worthy of Letitia.

Jon smiled and then it faded. "You're still dead set on figuring this out yourself?"

"I don't like the word dead," she said. "But fear not, I have a plan."

His eyebrows rose. "Care to share?"

"Not yet, no. Like you say, the less you're implicated, the better." She stroked Roberto's increasingly silky fur. "I'm sorry I dragged you into this. It's just... snakes? I mean, what are the chances that the biggest animal-phobe in this town should get caught up in an exotic pet mystery?"

"The irony isn't lost on me." He sipped his bourbon for a moment before asking, "What happened to put you off pets?"

"My mother. What else?" Her laugh was a bit shaky. "She can't stand mess of any kind, and told us cats and dogs carried viruses and parasites that could kill us. That's why I was so shocked when Nick moved here." She looked around her brother's living room, which was neither messy nor clean. It was just... normal. Somehow he'd emerged from their upbringing carrying far less baggage. "A town full of dogs sounded like trouble with a capital T." She tipped the last of the bourbon into her mouth and swallowed. "It's turned out to be true... for me, if not him."

"Pythons and giant guineas pigs are trouble?" he asked, trying to lighten the mood.

She looked down at the cat in her lap. "It's almost surreal." Rubbing her nose with a tissue, she added, "If it weren't for the allergies, I'd figure it's all a bad dream."

"It would be a dream come true for me, if this were all safe and legal. But it isn't. You don't know what you're up against. It could be a hobbyist, or far worse."

"My working theory is that it's a dog breeder," she said. "They're spooked by the prospect of tougher regulations that could cut their income. A lot of them are probably looking for a new revenue stream, and this sounds like a good one."

"A risky one," he said. "The Burmese python is not a snake for amateurs. At full growth, it can ingest a pig or even an alligator. They've been known to constrict handlers."

"Jon?" She brushed the cat off her lap and he hit the floor with an indignant mew. "Nightmares, remember? The last thing I need is a vision of an albino python eating a gator. Or a human for that matter."

"Some irresponsible owners have released them in Florida when they got too big. It's had a serious impact on the ecosystem. And yet people are still breeding, because people are still buying."

She got to her feet. "More bourbon?"

"I'm driving," he said. "You're driving."

"I'm walking," she said. "To the kitchen for more bourbon. And then home, where there are no pets."

"I'm taking the python and the capybara," he said. "Roberto is yours—mainly because I have the distinct impression he'd escape my place and come back to you. It's a long way."

"Just leave him the car keys," she said. "He tries to drive my car."

"I have a big van. Too much power for him."

She stood in the doorway waving the bourbon bottle. "Why? Why was he stuck between my doors? Why is he stuck on me, of all people?"

Jon got up and walked over. "You seriously underestimate your appeal. I mean, aside from the red nose, bloodshot eyes, and general air of hysteria."

"Very funny," she said, but she couldn't help grinning. A warm glow lit her up from inside that only partly came from the bourbon. "Thank you, Jon. I could not have handled this without you."

"Don't underestimate your abilities either," he said, picking up the terrarium. "I know you worry about your job, but it seems like that could go either way when there are politics at play."

"That's true. I just really want to turn my career around here." She stared at the floor. "And I don't want to embarrass my brother."

Nick had come to visit her after the fractured ribs, and one of the concussions. He teased her about being accident prone, but she knew he worried it was something worse. An illness, perhaps. She always laughed it off as a family curse that happened to skip him, unlike the red hair.

"I'm sure you never embarrass him," Jon said, starting to come toward her again.

She held up her hand. "Please. No closer with Butter-cup. I'll get Letitia into the plastic carrier."

When he got back from settling the snake in the van, he held the carrier at eye level. "Hey cutie. You'll love Gilda even more than Roberto. And I can't wait to study you."

Evie walked them to the door. "She's a chatterbox. I hope she doesn't keep you up."

"Luckily my tenants are away," he said. "Either way, you owe me. Dinner's on you once all this is over."

"Fair enough." This felt so far from over, she wondered if he'd ever get to collect. She waved as he got into his car, and Roberto sat between her feet, his tail coiled neatly around his paws. "Come on, buddy. I wasn't lying about having a plan. You and I have homework to do."

CHAPTER THIRTEEN

Mayor Bradshaw walked into the office just as Evie was about to walk out again. The clock in the tower had just chimed four, although it was probably closer to eight a.m. She had given up trying to predict the pattern. Some days it was more accurate than others.

"Evelyn, you're in early," he said. "Usually it's just me at this hour."

"So much to do, so little time, sir," she said. It was true, and giving up the capybara had given her more time to do it.

"I hardly ever see you," he said. "I hope you're well."

"Oh yes. I've just been getting out to explore the city and meet stakeholders. As you know, there's discontent brewing among dog breeders. I'm trying to figure out how to defuse it."

He raised broad shoulders in an elegant shrug. "I'm confident in our position. We can handle any fallout."

"Of course, sir. But why have any fallout if you can bring stakeholders into your camp instead?"

Slipping his arms out of the sleeves of his well-cut gray coat, he smiled. "I appreciate your enthusiasm, but don't tire yourself out on that particular hunt. You have bigger priorities."

"Bigger priorities?" What could be bigger than defusing another political scandal? Wasn't that why she was hired?

He opened the closet and looked back over his shoulder. "The Easter festival. You said it would unite people and I agreed with you. Dorset Hills loves a community event. It's our social glue."

"That was before I knew about the new policies you were introducing. The cat-lovers are starting to percolate, too."

"Cat-lovers. Seriously." He waved a hanger in her direction. "It's Dog Town. And I've been clear how I feel about cats. I can't even fill my bird feeder anymore. Worse than vermin."

"That's a little harsh, sir. Many citizens here love *all* animals, cats included."

"Well, they can love them inside. I don't know how they stand the shedding." He stroked his pristine coat before hanging it. "That's why I love poodles."

"Princess was a beautiful dog."

He turned quickly. "*Is* a beautiful dog. I would never give her up for good. She's just staying with friends out of state until this little kerfuffle about dog court dies down."

"Wouldn't it be great to settle the breeders, too, so that you and Princess can reunite?"

"We're on solid ground. Even the breeders agree there needs to be more oversight."

"True, but why rattle the bones when you don't have to? My goal is to keep your office out of the news... unless it's fabulous news."

His movie star smile reappeared, but she noticed it was dimmer than it had been in photos and footage and even his official portrait down the hall. Perhaps the political tempests had worn him down. "I like your spirit, Evelyn. But Zeke tells me this is all well in hand and I trust him implicitly."

"It just feels like something's simmering under the surface. I've been around politics long enough to know that doesn't usually end well."

The mayor's eyes closed for just a second, and when they opened, the lines on his face smoothed as if he'd been hit with Botox. "You're highly strung, Evelyn. That's understandable, given what's happened in your past. But you're in Dog Town now. Things don't really simmer here."

"I heard that things exploded over dog court and chicken-gate."

He flicked his fingers as if she were a gnat. "I remember it differently and you weren't here. Anyway, you need to die to the past, my dear. Every day is a new day."

Evie's lips almost twitched so she pressed them together. She'd learned to supress her true feelings years ago, even before entering the political realm. Nick called it "the dark art of fakery."

"Die to the past... Well, that sounds interesting."

"Let go, and let be. All will unfold as it should."

"I'll try to remember those words."

"More importantly, remember your breathing. It's the key to everything. You've got to learn to do it right. From the diaphragm."

"Homework," she said.

"Exactly." His eyes crinkled. "I want to use my platform to encourage mindfulness and I've got the perfect coach. It all boils down to this: *What you resist persists. What you embrace dissolves.*"

"So you're saying we shouldn't worry about the breeders at all? Even if they protest?"

"Just embrace the whole situation and see what happens," he said, heading to his office. "If you'll excuse me, I need to meditate before the day gets going."

Evie shook her head as she headed out of City Hall. Did he mean it? Was he taking a new medication? Or was someone medicating him on the sly? This didn't seem at all like the mayor she'd researched. The new, meditating mayor seemed like a lapdog when she'd expected a pit bull.

Sliding behind the wheel, she shook her head again. Aggressive dogs don't turn into sweethearts overnight, even with a new spiritual advisor on board. If she stopped resisting, he'd turn and pounce. Marti Forrester had told her as much, when she contacted the ousted dog court judge. Her exact words were: "Watch your back. Document everything. Have an exit strategy." Evie wished they could have had a long chat, but Marti had been texting from a beach in Baja, where she was detoxing from Dog Town. "You'll have allies," she'd said. "Trust them."

The allies hadn't been named but she knew Cori and Kinney had both helped Marti's bid to rescue her dog, Hank, from the clutches of dog court. It would be a relief to come clean with the mafia about what was happening with Roberto, but she wasn't totally convinced she could trust them yet. Not when the City was still paying her rent.

Passing the bronze St. Bernard and then the Dalmatian at the fire station, she headed back into her neighborhood. Instead of turning left onto her street, however, she made a right and another left before pulling up in front of a rundown house that had been a fine manor once. She parked the car in the street, grabbed her bag and walked up the driveway. One knock was all it took to start a cacophony inside. She'd expected the rich bass of large dogs—slobbery Newfies, perhaps, or menacing mastiffs.

Instead, the yapping came from small dogs, and plenty of them.

The door opened and Ruth Banks peeped out. There was a movement below as she swished dogs out of the way with her foot. Her gray hair was sleek and her sharp blue eyes blazed at the sight of Evie on her doorstep. Ruth had sat beside Leann at the City Hall breeders' meeting but she hadn't said much, and left early.

"What are *you* doing here?" she said. "Do you have a warrant?"

"A warrant! Ruth, I'm in public relations. I come in peace."

The door didn't open further. "You're in Bill Bradshaw's entourage. How peaceful can that be?"

"More peaceful than it used to be, from what I hear. Anyway, I just wanted to chat for a bit. I've been thinking about writing an article about you for the website."

"Me? Why?"

"Human interest. How many former zookeepers are running a breeding operation in Dorset Hills?"

"Just the one, to my knowledge. But I'm not interested in publicity, thank you."

Evie stared down, noticing white muzzles overlapping in the crack of the door. "You're not interested in promoting sales of your Maltese pups?"

"Not really. Most of us breed dogs for love, Evelyn. I want to further the breed and show them. Like the old saying goes, 'If you're making money breeding, you're doing something wrong.'"

"Those goals are mutually exclusive? Breeding for love *and* money?"

"Well, some think so." Finally the door opened wide enough to let Ruth slip out without releasing the pack.

"Honestly, I'm happy if I can make enough to buy quality breeding stock and keep the house in good shape."

Evie looked up at the peeling paint, a dangling eaves trough and eroding stonework. It had been decades since this house was in good shape.

"I don't see why you can't publicize your reputable breeding practice and still contribute to the breed."

Ruth leaned against the doorframe and crossed her arms. "Then you don't know breeders, do you? It's all about showing your passion and commitment at subsistence levels." She sighed and shrugged at the same time. "I tried to expand my business years ago, but it just stirred things up. It's better to go with the flow. I'm too old to fight."

"But you handled elephants. And seriously big cats. How can you let a few breeders scare you?"

Her silvery eyebrows drew in. "It takes a lot to scare me. I just can't be bothered with the infighting and backbiting." She looked up at the house again. "I don't make much, but I'll make even less when Bill Bradshaw limits the number of dogs I can own. If he sends his inspectors around, will this place pass the sniff test?"

"The goal isn't to stop legitimate breeders from producing dogs, Ruth. There's a demand for your pups, and if the supply dries up, people will start shopping outside of Dorset Hills. The mayor wouldn't want that. Nothing is set in stone, I assure you. Why don't you state your mind on the record?"

Now she laughed. "What I have to state about Bill Bradshaw wouldn't be printable. But since you're here, I'll make you a cup of tea and tell you what I really think. *Off the record.*"

Ruth held out her hand and Evie shook it. "Deal."

She stepped carefully into the house after Ruth to avoid

tripping over the dogs, and followed her to the kitchen. The place wasn't nearly as doggy as she'd expected. There was no smell, and it looked about as clean as her own house. She inhaled deeply and didn't even sneeze.

While the water heated, she joined Ruth at the sliding doors and stared out at the spacious back yard. There was a thick copse of spruce that cut off the rear of the property from view. If the breeder happened to be hiding secret pets, that was where they'd likely be.

"Are all the yards so deep around here?" Evie asked. "I'm only a few blocks away and we don't have nearly as much space."

"On Memorial Drive and a few other streets we have double lots, or even triple," Ruth said. "There's a ravine that limits development. That's why you'll find so many breeders in close proximity. There's enough room for outdoor pens—for those that have them—and plenty of trees to absorb sound and prevent noise complaints."

"And no limit on the number of dogs," Evie said, looking down. At least a dozen miniature white powder puffs danced around her feet.

"Not formally. Honestly, I think you'd find that most people self-regulate. I have space for 14 Maltese here. I would not have space for 14 St. Bernards. They'd be unhappy, I'd be unhappy and the neighbors would be *really* unhappy and complain to the City. So if that were my breed of choice, I'd only have six at a time. I'm not a fan of outdoor kennelling, although I don't knock breeders who do it. A St. Bernard might be happy living outside. My crew would be pupsicles."

Evie laughed. "I had you pegged for a large dog lady."

"My zoo days are over. I just want to be surrounded by puppies until I go to the big kennel in the sky. The more the better." She went back to the stove and turned the water off under the kettle. "Was that quotable enough for you?"

"You said we were off the record."

"Yeah, but I don't trust you." She poured water into the teapot, rinsed it, and poured again. After tossing in a couple of teabags, she covered it in a quilted dog-print tea cozy and then pinned Evie with her blue eyes. "Why are you really here?"

Perching on a stool at the counter, Evie said, "Intel gathering. I'm hoping you have some advice on defusing this situation before it—"

"Detonates?" She poured tea into two porcelain cups with matching saucers, and pushed one to Evie. "Because it will. Bill underestimates the wrath of dog breeders. I don't, because I've been bullied by them. Never in all my days working in cages with wild animals was I so unnerved as I am around a pack of breeders."

"Then why stay?"

Ruth shrugged. "It's the same everywhere. Nowadays you get trolled online. Your reputation can be shattered with a few anonymous lies in a breed forum. I've seen it happen often, and on a global scale."

"Wow." It came out on a deep sigh of disappointment. This coincided with what Ari had said, but she hadn't wanted to believe it was true across the board. "That sucks."

"It does indeed. There's no winning with trolls, so I do what I'm told or I find a darn good reason to abstain. Can't tell you how many times I've had to feign illness over the years to avoid one ruckus or another. People probably think I have a bad heart, and they'll start talking about that one day, too."

"So how can I quell this storm?"

"Best advice? Get the mayor to back right off. Let him

save face. The breeders will calm down, and what's more, they'll start regulating themselves more when you stop telling them they have to."

Evie sipped her tea. There was a lovely pattern of yellow roses and leaves on the china. Unlike the real thing, these roses had no thorns. "I don't think the mayor's willing to back off."

"Let me show you something." Ruth got up and left the kitchen.

When Evie heard her slow footsteps creaking up the stairs, she crept over and opened an old wooden door that led to the basement. Just a moment of silence was all it took to confirm there were no capybaras locked up down there. Three days with Letitia had taught her that a litter of giant guinea pigs couldn't stay quiet if they heard a noise.

Shutting the door quietly, she opened the patio doors and stepped onto the deck. Any outbuildings would have to be thoroughly soundproofed to keep the neighbors in the dark about exotic animals.

"Everything check out?" Ruth asked, standing in the doorway with her laptop.

"Just admiring your landscaping," Evie said, coming back inside. "Any advice on how to guide the CCD around spot-checking operations without being heavy handed?"

Ruth set the laptop on the counter and beckoned. She pointed to a series of defamatory comments directed at Arianna Torrance by posters with names like "DogPurist" and "GoldensFurever."

"That's terrible!" Evie's heart ached for sweet Ari and her sweeter dogs. Thurston Howl didn't deserve this kind of vitriol.

"Some of these people are from Dog Town and others

from far beyond," Ruth said. "So no, Evie, I can't tell you how to spot-check other breeders."

Tipping back the last of the tea, Evie said, "Understood. I'm sorry I asked." She blinked a few times. "And I'm really sorry I looked at that forum. My eyes feel dirty."

"Welcome to the wild and wonderful world of dog breeding, young lady."

CHAPTER FOURTEEN

Evie was still patching up the scratches on her hands when she heard the thump at her back door. She hadn't expected Roberto to create such a fuss. He'd seemed like the kind of cat who wouldn't mind carrying a camera around the neighborhood attached to his collar. Turns out she had misjudged him. She'd prevailed at last, and after falling over dramatically a couple of times, the cat decided he could get around just fine and went out into the night. Whether he'd visit his furry and scaled friends was anyone's guess, but it seemed like that was part of his evening rounds. If he wasn't going to take her to them physically, he could take her along virtually.

"Back so soon?" she said, opening the door to let him in. He staggered past her, pretending again that the burden of the camera was too great. "How come you only spy when you feel like it and not when I want you—"

The last word was cut off by a loud screech, and it didn't come from her. Roberto dropped something brown and furry on the floor at her feet. It screeched again, and then her screech overlapped. Whatever it was took off across the kitchen with an odd gait that was half-run, half-hop. Roberto recovered his elegance instantly and with two leaps, landed on the creature again. It gave a muffled squawk and collapsed. He draped himself over it and stared up at her as if to say, "Now what?"

"Not again! All I wanted you to do was poke around and get me some footage."

Scrambling over to the sink, she opened the cupboard underneath. Inside was a blue plastic washtub. She carried it back to the cat and maneuvered it into position over him.

"Okay. On the count of three, you're going to move and I'm going to trap that thing. Got it? One... two... three!"

Roberto darted aside and she slammed down the plastic tub before the creature even realized it was free.

"Okay. Okay," she said, panting. "Well, you know the drill, Roberto." She grabbed her phone off the counter and then placed one sneaker firmly on the blue tub. She pressed the numbers, and when Jon picked up, she put the phone on speaker and set it on the floor. Better to keep both hands free.

"Are you okay?" he asked. "You sound far away."

"The phone's on the floor, so that I can be ready for whatever happens next."

"Uh-oh. What is it now?"

"I don't know. I don't know what it is, Jon. It was small and gold, about the size of a football with a long tail. I think I saw big eyes. I definitely saw claws."

"Where did it go?"

"I caught it!" She knew she sounded like a proud kid. "It's under a tub."

"Well done," he said, almost laughing, but not quite. "Now you've got to get it secured. I can't keep anything more at my place. The capy never freaking shuts up."

"I know, right? But this thing has a set of lungs too. I can't keep it here."

His sigh wafted up from the phone on the floor. "Okay. I'll be there soon, and we'll take it to your brother's place."

That was all he said, but it was the way he said it. She knew she was pushing his patience. He owed her nothing, really. This was all out of the goodness of his heart for the sake of the animals.

"Thanks, Jon. I can't even tell you how much I appreciate it."

"Hold your position, soldier," he said, hanging up.

***

"KINKAJOU!" Jon sounded almost joyful when he peeked into the tub with his flashlight.

"Pardon me?"

"It's a kinkajou—a honey bear. It comes from South America and is part of the raccoon family. They're mischievous and nocturnal. Good thing I brought a big crate."

"You sound a little too happy about this," Evie said. "My brother is not going to be thrilled to have a honey bear subletting his place. Does this thing stink or is something rotting in the kitchen?"

"It's a bit musky. Not too bad."

"If I can smell it despite allergies, it's not too good, either."

Jon readied the huge dog crate he'd brought over in his truck. "I'll have to run out and get some fruit. The name comes from its sweet tooth. They love figs and dates, and swing through the rainforest using prehensile tails."

Jon looked like a kid in a candy shop. For the moment, he'd blocked out the reason for the honey bear's visit.

Only later, after he'd settled the creature and brought back supplies, did reality set in. He sat across from Evie at Nick's kitchen table and the excitement drained out of him. He wasn't much older than she was, but he looked it, suddenly. "This just gets worse and worse. Evie, please tell me you're ready to call animal control. Heaven only knows what Roberto will bring home next."

The cat jumped up on the table at his name and sat between them. It appeared that he considered himself an integral part of the conversation.

"Roberto, would you mind?" she said. "I know where those paws and jaws have been."

"Oh, it's okay. It's not like we're eating." Jon ran his hand over the cat and fiddled with his collar. "Hey. What's this?"

"A video camera for cats," she said. "I'm hoping it'll show us where he went tonight."

Jon stared at her. "You put a spy cam on your cat?"

"Not my cat. But yes, I put a camera on Roberto. Obviously he wants to help. Otherwise he wouldn't keep bringing home rescues."

"It doesn't feel right to put him in the middle of all this deliberately," Jon said. "He's just a cat who showed up at your door."

"Between my doors, if you recall. Like he was put there for a reason."

Jon shook his head. "The point is that a camera draws attention to him. Do you think someone breeding and selling rare creatures would ignore that?"

She looked at the cat sheepishly and Roberto stared back. If he could shrug, he would. "I'm assuming Bert knows how to handle himself. He's been getting in and out of this place on his own without being seen."

"Well, the camera would make that more difficult. It's unwieldy."

"He was agile enough to catch the honey bear and carry it back, even with the camera."

Roberto fell over on his side and the camera thunked on the table. She glared at him, certain the move was to get Jon's sympathy.

"Evie. I understand what's at stake for you, really I do. But we can't let this get too far out of hand. It's not fair to Roberto."

"Roberto," she said. "Tell Jon you *want* to play detective. He's not listening to me."

The cat got up and went over to rub his head under the vet's jaw. Back and forth he went, purring.

"How'd you train him to do that?" Jon asked, removing the collar.

"He's not your average cat." She got up to collect her laptop from her bag. "Let's watch the footage."

Jon didn't protest again as she connected the cat's collar to her computer. "It probably won't even work," she said. "The reviews were iffy. Apparently, the dog-sized cameras work better."

A shaky image appeared on the screen, and she moved around the table and angled the screen so that Jon could see, too. Right away she recognized her street even in the waning light. Roberto wove his way east, dodging in and out of trees and behind parked cars. It was dizzying and she had to close her eyes for a moment. When she opened them again, he was crossing a street on a green light. On the other side, he turned left and trotted along the fence. All the joggling suggested he was running now. It wasn't his usual fluid movement. He crossed another street and then another, and her stomach knotted. He negotiated traffic so well, but you could never depend on erratic drivers.

"That's Memorial Drive," she said. "I was there today and I saw that old green VW van on the road."

Roberto didn't stop at Ruth's house. He ran past, and then turned at least once more. After that, it was hard to see anything. It was like he was in deep bush. That segment of video went on for what felt like ages, and then suddenly, it was light again. Not bright, but lighter. It seemed that he was inside, now, weaving among metal dog crates lined up on the floor. There were bodies small or large in each one, but as the creatures bunched together, it was impossible to identify the inhabitants. Squeaks and clicks and chirring sounds came from the laptop, and Roberto pawed at the keyboard. Evie wasn't sure whether he wanted to turn it up or silence it. On screen the video spun in dizzying ways. It was as if the cat was doing gymnastics. Suddenly a bright light shone, and the image went still. After a few moments, it activated again. The light was low and there was a blurred swoop and a metallic rattle, as if Roberto had jumped onto something. He turned and the camera caught a clear view of what appeared to be more than a dozen crates. Light bounced off some glass containers as well. Then everything went black.

"No," Evie said, jabbing at the computer keys. "We almost had it."

Jon let her try for a few minutes and then gently took her hand. "The camera went offline, Evie. He must have knocked it askew."

"But we have no idea where he was."

"Maybe not exactly, but we're better off than we were before. We know it's not so far from Memorial Drive. And we've seen cages filled with chirping animals." He rested his elbows on the table and his face in his hands. "This is bigger than I feared."

She threw herself back in the wooden chair, disappointed. "Now what do I do?" She held up one palm as he started to speak. "Other than call animal services, I mean."

"What you *don't* do is put this cat at further risk," he said pushing the chair back and rising. "I'll be back tomorrow night to check on the honey bear. If you have a plan, I look forward to hearing it. If not, I'm surrendering the honey bear myself and trying to explain the situation as best I can."

She stared after him in silence as he walked to the back door.

"Maybe I should take the cat, too," he said.

"Good luck with that. This cat makes his own decisions."

"Hmmm," was his only response as he gathered his things.

She realized after the words were out that it sounded pretty stupid, but she wasn't taking them back. Just because they sounded stupid didn't mean they weren't true.

Roberto climbed into her lap after the door closed, and she ran her hand over his back. His fur was already softer because of the good quality kibble she fed him. "Never mind him, little buddy," she said, scratching behind his ears. "You did great. You're a Secret Agent Feline."

CHAPTER FIFTEEN

The honey bear was making odd yodelling sounds from his cage when she arrived at Nick's house after work the next day, but it seemed happy enough, especially after she dropped some dates and figs between the bars.

"You look like a Winifred," she said, smiling as Roberto purred and arched his back to greet the honey bear. "Do you agree, Roberto?" He offered assent by doing a figure eight between her ankles. "Good. Winnie it is."

"Winnie? I think he might take issue with that, considering he's a boy." Jon had used the key she gave him to let himself in. His grin was infectious and his judgmental tone of the previous night had vanished. "How about Wilber?"

Roberto took his displays of affection to Jon's ankles, so she said, "I guess that's a yes."

"Evie, I'm sorry I got so short last night. Honestly, I'm just mad at myself for getting deeper into this than I should have for my own comfort. I'm normally a play-it-by-the-rules kind of guy."

"I understand," she said. "And if you have to back out,

that's okay too. Just please let me figure this out on my own."

He slung his backpack onto the counter and came over. "You're not going to be able to give this cat up, are you?"

She shrugged. "Depends on my allergies and the offers I get." She smiled as the cat's ears pressed back against his head. "He is growing on me."

"I knew it. Allergies or no allergies, you're a consummate cat lady."

"Excuse me? I am many things, but a 'consummate cat lady' is not one of them."

He leaned over the honey bear's crate, still grinning. "You misunderstand me. Where I come from, that's the consummate compliment."

"Where *do* you come from? Remind me not to go there."

"I come from Dorset Hills. Born and bred, with little experience of the normal world," he said, now on his knees. "I'm not worldly, like you."

"If you weren't doing me a huge favor, I'd be getting huffy right about now," she said. "But I'll leave this to you, Dr. Doolittle."

She moved quickly as he flipped the latch on the cage. The mild-mannered, big-eyed creature reminded her a bit of a monkey, and she didn't want to be too close when it was free. Roberto paced back and forth between rooms. His tail twitched, as if he had a bone to pick with someone. Probably her, for not being more attentive.

Opening her laptop, she checked on her work e-mails. Zeke and the mayor had been out on some secret mission all day. It was annoying. How was she supposed to do a good job if they were always keeping her in the dark? On the other hand, with the mayor behaving as if he'd been force-fed yoga pills, maybe she should stay out of it. She had nothing against yoga, per se, but always considered it wise to have a healthy skepticism of anything that captured the zeitgeist... including dogs.

Her computer beeped an alert, and she clicked automatically on Nick's Skype message. His smile stretched across the screen. "Hey sis."

"Hi there! How's work going?"

"Good. Work's always good. I'm a rock star, remember?"

"How could I forget when you're always reminding me?"

He laughed. "Good thing you're my twin. Eventually it will spill over to you, too."

She smiled back. "Can't wait. I wanna be a rock star, too."

"I know you do." Leaning into the screen, he added. "I see you're hanging out at my place to catch good vibes. I told you your rental is a dump."

"You did, and you were right. Still can't figure out how the cat gets out. The contractor was baffled. He's coming back next week with a team."

"Maybe you should buy the place. Then you can gut it and catproof it."

The idea would have been ridiculous a few weeks ago. Now, despite all that had happened, staying longer in Dorset Hills had more appeal. So much that she didn't bother to protest. "In the meantime, I worry about him."

"He's a cat. He'll land on his paws. And if not, well, he has nine lives. Just like you, apparently."

"Funny." She peeked into the dining room and saw Jon was still on his knees. The honey bear was sitting on his shoulder while he cleaned out the cage. "I might need a few more lives to get it right."

Nick sat up straighter and his face shifted on the screen. "Why? What's going on? Are you keeping your nose clean like I told you?"

"Actually, you said to watch my back."

"Well, *are* you? Because Zeke called to see how you were doing."

She rubbed her forehead, wondering how long she'd had the headache that suddenly seemed horrendous. "He called *you* to see how I was doing?"

"Well, yeah. I'm your big brother. He said you never complain, even though you got stuck into some tough issues."

Her hackles dropped and the headache eased immediately. "There's a tempest brewing in the Dog Town teapot."

"That's just business as usual. Don't let it get to you." He started rolling his shoulders, a classic Nick sign of fading interest. "How's the house?"

"Fine." She had cleaned up the bathtub after the capybara, but now the air was heavy with honey bear musk. "All good, brother."

"Yeah? Because my neighbor texted to say he'd heard screaming coming from the direction of my house. I figured it was nothing to worry about, but thought I'd better check."

"Maybe if I tripped over the cat. He comes with me when I collect the mail." She summoned her special political smile that could fake out even her brother. "Everything's good."

"Okay then, I'd better go and—whoa! Jon, is that you?"

The veterinarian had come up behind her and then backed quickly away. Sheepishly, he stepped into camera range. Luckily the honey bear wasn't with him.

"Hey, Nick. How's Clive?"

"Amazing, as always." Nick's eyebrows had notched up and stayed there. "So, I guess that explains the screaming. You're having a party while I'm gone. Go easy on my sister, buddy."

"Nick!" Evie turned to Jon. "I'm so sorry. My parents gave him to wolves as an infant."

"And they gave Evie to unicorns," Nick said.

"I love unicorns," Jon said, grinning. "Anyway, I just came to visit Roberto. To see how his abscess is doing."

Nick was fully alert now. All signs of boredom had vanished. "Huh. A house call. At *my* house. Interesting."

"It's not what you're thinking," Evie said. "Jon has been providing excellent service—"

"That's *exactly* what I was thinking."

She put her hand over the laptop camera to block Nick. "Never mind. You said you had to get going."

"Yeah, but seeing Jon reminds me... I've been checking into that skull you gave me."

"Skull?" Jon asked, gently prying her fingers off the camera.

"She didn't tell you? The one she dug up on the Dayton estate."

"I didn't dig it up. Remi's dog did. When we were scouting for the Easter hunt."

Jon leaned closer to the screen to see the skull Nick was holding up. "It looks like a cat. A big one."

"Right?" Nick's face was fully animated. "Like a jaguar."

"Too small," Jon said.

"A small jaguar," Nick said.

Jon laughed. "More like an ocelot. Send me some pics?"

"Sure. And when I get back, we can compare notes."

If they'd been dogs, their tails would have been lashing furiously. Evie couldn't help but smile. Jon's expression was usually so serious. Seeing him geek out like that made him even more appealing.

Nick caught her look. "Have you told Jon about the curse, Evie?"

"A curse?" Jon said. "That sounds more interesting than an ocelot's skull."

Evie leaned in to make sure her brother got the full benefit of her glare. "Never mind, Nick."

"Your call, sis. I think it's only fair to the man, if he's making house calls. Unless Zeke is still a contender."

"Zeke? *What?* Nick, don't even."

"Can't see why else Zeke would be calling me. Putting in a good word with your big brother."

There was a reason she'd tried to keep Nick from meeting the guys she dated. Largely, she'd been successful, but he'd visited and even helped her move a few times, so he'd crossed paths with a few of her boyfriends. During her short stint in Seattle, he'd met Ryan the mountain climber, and in San Francisco, he met Graham, the diver. Both men had been smart, and decent, but it was hard to remember them as individuals after her brother started calling them "Surf and Turf." She didn't want Jon to suffer the same fate, since the two men were permanent Dog Town residents.

"Nick, can we not talk about my love life?" she pleaded.

"There's a skull in my hand and it reminds me of your graveyard of buried boyfriends. How can I stop?"

"Because the next skull in *my* hand could be yours. The curse isn't picky, brother."

He laughed. "Just stop thinking so much. You're making my head hurt."

"Your head would hurt even more if you walked a mile in my shoes."

"That's not all that would hurt," he said. "My pride would take a real hit if I wore your pumps around town."

Jon shook his head. "You two are making me glad I'm an only child."

"Let's pretend I am," she said, slamming the laptop shut.

CHAPTER SIXTEEN

Jon crossed his arms and leaned against the kitchen counter. "Were you going to mention this skull at some point? It must have occurred to you that it could be linked to the current situation." He gestured at the honey bear, which was in it's cage, busily extracting treats from a hard plastic dog toy.

"I had forgotten all about it, honestly." She shook her head, perplexed. "Nick didn't think much of it at the time so I didn't connect them. I guess I'm not much of an investigator." Getting up from the table, she started pacing. "Do you really think it's an ocelot?"

"Hard to say. I'd need to study it. But it's definitely something to look into, because we haven't had a wildcat sighting of any kind for at least a decade. The real question is, how long was it buried? If it's reasonably recent, then maybe it's related."

Evie shuddered. "I don't even want to think about it."

"Does that mean you're sending me alone?"

She closed her eyes and focused on her breath, just like

the mayor had told her. "You want to see what we can dig up?"

"Literally. Yes."

She could hear the smile in his voice, even with her eyes closed. "I'm glad you can still see some humor in this situation."

"It's hard not to. At the moment, it seems too absurd to be true. And yet... we have to consider that it might be."

"I didn't want it to be true," she said. "I guess I've been in denial." She opened her eyes, and Nick's kitchen looked somehow different. Everything was exactly as it had been, but it seemed like the light was different. It was as if a cool blue filter had slipped over her retinas. "Time to face reality."

"You okay?" He crossed the kitchen and rested a hand on her shoulder. It felt warm and heavy and calming. Better than a yoga pill.

"Yeah. Let's go check it out."

"Now?" He glanced at her black shirt and heels, and it struck her that his eyes lingered longer than strictly necessary given the task at hand. "It's past nine."

"You're hiding a capybara and a python and I'm stinking my brother's place out with a kinkajou. The sooner we get to the bottom of this, the better."

Jon lifted his shoulders in surrender. "Does your brother have a shovel?"

"Check the shed out back while I find something else to wear."

A few minutes later, they met back in the kitchen. His eyes once again took her in, and this time he fought a smile. She'd rolled her brother's trackpants up over her ankles and topped them with his faded university sweatshirt.

"The heels might be a problem," Jon said, the smile

winning. "It's been raining. How are you going to walk over sodden grass in stilettos?"

"You'd be surprised at what I can accomplish in stilettos," she said. "But luckily I have a pair of old sneakers in the car."

They fell silent on the short drive. Jon's profile was as serious as she'd ever seen it, and even when some whooping teens ran a stop sign and cut him off, he stayed cool. That calm spilled over to her, and she soaked in as much as she could.

He parked well back from the parking lot, and got out of the car.

"There will be security cameras," he said, opening the rear door of the van to get the shovel and his backpack. "We'll need to walk through the bush and keep to the back of the property."

"You're bringing Gilda?" she asked, as the dog paced behind them.

"Yep. She'll be the first to notice any trouble."

Evie didn't want to know what kind of trouble he had in mind, but she liked the idea of having the big dog along—especially when Gilda stuck to her side instead of his. It was as if she knew well who most needed comfort.

Jon led the way in silence, reaching out now and then to hold back branches or steady her. The further they got from the car, the darker it got. He used the light on his phone, but kept it low to avoid detection. When he stopped to get his bearings, Evie stared up at the sky. It was clear and vast, and filled with more stars than she could ever see in the places she'd lived before. Or maybe she'd never really looked.

"This way," he said.

"We'll never make it," she said, in a moment of panic. "It's a jungle."

"Of course we will." He slid his hand down her arm and closed his fingers around hers. "I used to run all over the grounds with my friends when I was a kid. Before it was a City landmark."

It eased her mind to think he knew the terrain that well, but she didn't let go of his hand even after they were through the bush and picking their way through the statues to the rear of the mansion. The figures were eerie by day, and terrifying by night. "If I were alone, I'd... Well, I'd never come here alone in the dark," she whispered. "Not for all the exotic animals in the world."

"It'll be okay," he said, finally releasing her hand. "We'll only stay 10 minutes... as long as you can remember where you found the skull."

"It was just south of the faun and east of the gorgon," she said.

"The faun is...?"

"The one with small horns and cloven hooves."

"And the gorgon?"

"Headful of snakes," she said, reaching for his hand again. "Pythons, maybe."

He shone the light around. "Horns. Check. Snake wig... *whoa*."

"Right? How could you forget?"

"We were young. Strong hearts."

She led him to the garden at the rear of the property. He handed her the light and dropped his backpack on the wet grass. Kneeling, he pulled out a trowel, a brush, and a couple of garbage bags.

"There," she said. "You can still see the hole Leo dug, even after the rain."

Squatting, Jon used the trowel to move the soil carefully. She stood over him, shining the light. Every so often the beam would hit the silver trowel and blind her for a second.

After a few minutes of prodding the dirt, Jon said, "It *was* what Nick thought."

"What do you mean?" Nick thought a lot of things, most of them garbage. "I don't follow."

"When you told him, 'it's not what you think.'"

Her brain struggled to piece it together. "It's not what you think...? Oh. *Oh*."

He was silent for another minute, and the smell of damp soil rose around him. "I wouldn't be out here digging for just anyone," he said at last.

"Not even for a jaguar?" she asked.

The trowel paused. "I'd love to see a jaguar." The digging resumed. "Alive, I mean."

She waited a beat, wondering if she should encourage him. Obviously, she shouldn't. This was too nice a man to curse. But on the other hand, he'd been well and thoroughly warned by her brother, and a grown man could make his own decisions. Finally she spoke. "Are you saying this is our first date, Jon? Because the ambience leaves a lot to be desired."

His shoulders shook. "A guy likes to make an impression."

"Mission accomplished. I will never forget the gorgon at night. Or the stars overhead. No one does stars like Dorset Hills."

"Light, Evie. Focus." When she'd lifted her eyes, the light had bounced around crazily, hitting various statues.

"You're the one who got off topic."

"Just wanted to lighten the mood." His shoulders shook again, and she laughed, too. Quietly, so as not to awaken the sleeping mythological creatures.

"Tell you what," she said. "You propose a more traditional setting for a date, and we'll talk about it." The light bobbed around a bit in her hand. "Like my brother said, there's some history you need to know."

"Oh?"

Just then there was a clunk, of metal on stone.

Or bone.

"What is it?"

He reached up and took the phone out of her hand so that he could direct it into the hole. "Evie, just look away."

"At what? The gorgon, or the faun or the satyr?"

"Anything is better than this. Just step out of the light and I'll manage."

She leaned over and took the phone back. "Thank you. But no. I got you into this, and I'm sticking it out."

Her right hand directed the light steadily, while the fingers of her left stroked Gilda's ears. The dog had kindly offered her head for that purpose.

Half an hour later, they walked back to the van. Jon was carrying two garbage bags, so she continued to rest her hand on Gilda. It was a comfort, given what she'd seen.

They drove in silence again, and when Jon turned into her driveway, he asked, "So... worst date ever?"

She thought about it. "Actually, no. One time, a guy accidentally backed into me in my own driveway. We spent six hours in emergency."

"Wow. Why wasn't he walking you to the door?"

"He'd honked for me to come out before the date. I guess that was my first sign." She laughed uneasily. "When I miss the first sign, the second usually hits harder."

"No one expects to get run over on a date."

"I never rule it out. Like Nick says, there's a curse."

He turned the key and the engine died. "I'm a man of science, Evie. I don't believe in curses."

"Says the man with bags of bones in his trunk."

"Well, that's not ideal, but it's not the result of a curse."

"Maybe not. But my relationships rarely end well." She stared at her hands, and then glanced over at him. "It's only fair you should know."

"Duly noted." A slow smile spread over his face. "How about we take it one date at a time and just see what happens. I promise it won't be all honey bears and pet cemeteries."

"Okay," she said. "If you're willing to take the risk..."

"I am." He made a move as if to put his hand on her knee, and seeing the dark crescents under his nails, thought better of it.

She took his hand anyway, and his fingers twined through hers. No one had ever wrangled animals, dead or alive, for her before. It wasn't the worst date ever. On the contrary, it might just be the best. Even with Gilda resting her dirty damp muzzle on her shoulder.

Jon leaned in, pulling her toward him at the same time. She resisted for a second or two, knowing she shouldn't, yet aching for the comfort of a warm embrace. It had been too long since anyone had hugged her, and it might just be the only thing that knocked the image of what they'd found that night out of her mind. His hand slid up her arm to her shoulder and then her neck, sending a cascade of tingles like little starbursts down her spine. She didn't remember feeling anything like that with Surf and Turf, or anyone else for that matter. It must be the Dog Town effect. Time seemed to slow down so she could notice every sensation.

He leaned closer and hesitated, just long enough to make her worry he was changing his mind.

That was when a sudden thump made them both jump and gasp. She turned to see two green eyes staring in at them through the windshield, and an orange striped tail lashing. The movement had activated the motion detector light and obliterated all the tingly starbursts.

"Roberto! Good grief, he escaped again."

Jon's laugh was as warm as an audible hug. "He must dissolve into mist and float through cracks."

"What's that on his collar?" she asked, opening the passenger door.

Roberto strolled out of reach and they circled him on either side of the car. Before he could leap away, Evie grabbed him and plucked a twist of blue paper from his collar.

The cat placed his front paws onto her shoulders and started headbutting her as she unravelled the note.

"What does it say?" Jon asked.

"Keep your cat at home," Evie read. *"Or else."*

CHAPTER SEVENTEEN

K inney Butterfield's warm smile was missing in action when she walked into Evie's office the next afternoon.

"Did you click your heels to get here that fast?" Evie asked. She'd barely finished texting her request to meet the canine corrections officer. "I just pressed send."

Checking her phone, Kinney said, "Actually, I hadn't noticed. That's not why I'm here."

"Oh? What's going on?"

"There's a demonstration outside. About 60 dog breeders are marching around the German shepherd statue with placards."

"Uh-oh. Does the mayor know?"

"Security's on it, and notified the mayor and Zeke."

Evie let out a little of the air she'd sucked in. "Okay, good."

"Not so good. Zeke wants you to handle it."

"He told you that?"

Kinney held up her phone so Evie could read his text:

"Evelyn knows this issue best. She'll be on point to help disperse the crowd."

"Is he kidding?" She pushed back her chair and stood up. "I haven't even seen the draft regulations. Where is he?"

"Off site, apparently. Security saw Zeke's red convertible pull out about half an hour ago. Maybe someone tipped them off."

Evie checked her phones and computer just to confirm there were no messages. When she looked up, Kinney's eyes were full of sympathy.

"All right, then," Evie said, grabbing her jacket. "Let's see how hungry the wolves are today."

They walked through City Hall together, Evie's heels tapping on the marble tiles. If things continued on the way they had, she'd have to rethink her footwear. Maybe stilettos had no place in Dog Town. Kinney's boots were the more sensible choice. If heads had to roll, she'd be ready to drop-kick them.

"What are you going to say?" Kinney asked.

"No idea. Hoping inspiration will strike when I get there."

"The crowd's pretty hot right now. You'll need to tread lightly."

"Understood." She turned to Kinney. "I can't believe my bosses threw me under the bus."

Kinney kept her expression neutral. "I know the mayor's been keeping it chill. Trying to ride out recent hits."

Evie sighed. "I shouldn't be so surprised, I guess. My business cards say 'Professional Scapegoat.'"

"I know what that feels like. I was set up to fail in this job, too."

"It's not fair," Evie said. "I came to Dorset Hills because I thought it would be different. Kinder."

"It is different." Kinney checked over her shoulder. "Kinder, maybe not. Or at least, kindness doesn't look like you'd expect. It's there, though. You just need to pick your way through landmines to find it."

"Sorry to whine," Evie said. "After all, I chose this line of work. I know I get hired so that politicians have someone to fire. When you look at it that way, I've actually been quite successful."

Kinney laughed, and then stopped. "Sorry."

"Don't be. Laughter is all that keeps me going some days."

"I hear you. Someone probably should have warned you that everything you experienced elsewhere is just magnified and distorted in Dog Town."

"Nick never said that."

"Maybe he doesn't experience it that way. In the tech realm, he's somewhat removed."

"It's more than that. My brother has always moved easily through life. Crowds part. People smile before he says a word. He doesn't always see stuff like this, which is a relief sometimes. But he did say enough to alert me and I didn't pay attention. I guess I wanted to believe in Dog Town's magic."

"Me too. I came here full of hope and expectation and it's been letting me down ever since." She turned at the door. "On the political side, that is. Underneath, there's a vein of gold. Remember that."

"Vein of bronze. Got it."

Kinney laughed again, pausing with her hand on the knob on one of the old oak doors. "Keep on schticking. You ready?"

"Hit it."

There was a bellow from the crowd as someone recognized her.

"Hit it!" someone shouted.

Kinney and Evie glanced at each other and actually laughed. Maybe the laugh fanned the crowd's ire, because the placards soared higher above heads and a chant began. "Back off Breeders... Back off Breeders."

"Yeah," Evie muttered. "Back *off*, breeders."

"Patience," Kinney said. "Humor."

Evie picked her way carefully down the uneven front stairs, noticing the chant got louder with each step. On the last one, she stopped and raised her arm. "Good afternoon, everyone."

Her words were swallowed in the din, but someone raised a megaphone. "Quiet. I saw her lips move."

The chant subsided, and Evie began. "The mayor asked me to speak to you today."

Instantly the yelling resumed. "Bring us the mayor. Bring us the mayor."

Evie waited, knowing they wouldn't miss an opportunity to speak to someone, even if it was just the professional scapegoat. Sure enough, after a minute or so, the voices trailed off.

"I want to hear all about your concerns," she said. "I offered to establish a committee, but none of you came forward."

"You don't really care," someone shouted. "It's just poop bag politics."

"Poop bag politics," the crowd chanted. They liked that one and it carried on for a good few minutes.

Finally, Evie turned to make an elaborate false exit. That usually shut people up fast.

"Hey, poop bagger," someone shouted. "Why can't the mayor stay out of our backyards? Dog breeders helped put this town on the map. People all over North America buy our dogs."

Evie turned back to face Leann Cosgrove. "I agree with you. A dog bred in this city is a collector's item. I met people in California with two or three Dog Town originals."

"My hounds have bloodlines dating back to the Dayton family," Leann said. "For an outsider like you, that's one of the founders of Dorset Hills."

"Practically royalty, I know," Evie said. "So, who nominates Leann as official spokesperson for the dog breeders of Dorset Hills?"

The murmur of assent collided with the murmur of dissent. It pretty much neutralized the vote.

"Thanks, but no thanks," Leann said. "I don't engage in poop bag politics."

"It's hard to put yourself on the frontlines," Evie said. "But someone has to speak for your group." Her eyes scanned the crowd, hoping to see Ari's blonde hair. "Other takers?"

A few people shoved Leann forward and she struggled against them. A bald man wearing loose, flowing pants and floral socks under sandals emerged from the crowd. "I'll stand by you, Leann. We'll do it together."

Evie came down the stairs and the man said, "Are those snakeskin shoes?"

She looked down at her pumps, uncertainly. They'd been a deal in a California outlet mall. "Knock offs," she said.

"I call BS," he said. "We can't trust anyone who'd wear dead snakes. First, snakeskin shoes, then snake oil politics."

The breeders picked up on that and started hissing, "Snakeskin shoes, snake oil politics."

Evie thought about the albino python she'd saved and felt a prickle of resentment. If they had any idea...

Maybe Kinney saw a change in her posture, because she came down the steps. Standing on the second from the bottom, she called, "Quiet."

It was like she'd hit mute on a remote. A dog cop clearly had more clout than a public relations person with this mob. Understandable, when a spot check from the CCD could put them out of business instantly. Kinney handed her phone to Evie, so that she could read the text from Zeke.

Evie stepped up beside her before addressing the crowd again. "I've heard that the CCD's been getting calls about breeders on the Tattle Tail hotline," Evie said. "Calls letting the City know about breeders who aren't necessarily working for the dogs' greater good." Outrage brought the loudest shouts yet, but Evie waited them out. "Here's the thing," she said, when they quieted. "Some of those calls came from other breeders."

Complete silence fell as this sank in.

"That proves my point," Evie said. "You'll be stronger if you work together, rather than sabotaging each other. My door is open when you're ready to dig in."

As she walked back up the stairs, the shouting began again, but this time the din was chaotic and jumbled as the protesters all turned on one other.

EVIE SETTLED into the passenger seat of Kinney's Prius. "Thanks for driving me home. I left my car at my brother's last night."

"No problem," Kinney said. "You shouldn't be walking alone until tempers settle. People with an ax to grind take any opportunity."

Evie checked her phone again for word from the mayor or Zeke. Usually the people throwing her to the dogs had the decency to thank her—before they fired her. "I don't agree with Zeke's strategy," she said. "Pitting the breeders against each other *is* poop bag politics, in my opinion. They'll come back stronger and more suspicious."

"Typical political move," Kinney said. "Do what works now and think of the future later."

"The future involves offering me up on a silver platter, I suppose."

"You're not going down without a fight, I hope."

Evie turned and grinned. "Never. I'm always kicking and screaming as the final curtain falls."

"I admire your spirit, I really do. I hope they won't beat it out of you like they did Marti Forrester."

"I'm made of sterner stuff," Evie said. "Or maybe not, but I've been on the frontlines longer than Marti was. It helps knowing that this is my last political job."

"Oh?" Kinney steered the Prius through the foot traffic around the St. Bernard outside the hospital. Judging by the photos on social media, this was the most popular of the bronze dogs with the tourists who came into town by the busload to see them.

"I moved here wanting a fresh start. I didn't intend to work with the City, but I fell into it because of Nick's connections. And it was what I knew." She traced her finger around the side window as she stared out. "Dog Town isn't as unassuming as it looks in photos."

"No, but it's interesting," Kinney said, smiling. "And I

have the feeling you've got something fascinating to tell me."

Evie nodded. "Fascinating, yes. I hope I can trust you, Kinney, because I haven't exactly been following professional protocol."

"I've been known to color outside the lines myself," Kinney said, turning right at the fire station's Dalmatian and then slowing to a crawl so that she could pay close attention to Evie's tale. "I bet this has something to do with Roberto the Red."

"It does. If I knew who stuck him between my doors…" Her voice almost cracked. "Well, I don't know what I'd do, because that cat has grown on me and now someone's threatening him."

Kinney pulled over, put the car in park, and turned on the flashers. "Tell me."

Evie didn't spare a single detail. Kinney listened intently, and her expression barely changed until she heard about the bags of bones now residing in Nick's back shed, only because neither Evie nor Jon had sheds, and neither one wanted them in the house. At this, Kinney closed her eyes and rubbed her forehead. "Oh crap," she said. "This isn't good."

"It most certainly is not," Evie agreed. "The mayor will flip, and then he'll fire me before I've even fulfilled my role as professional scapegoat."

"But then he'll bungle the whole thing and it'll be worse for Dog Town. And possibly even for the exotic pets someone is breeding illegally."

"And now this person is threatening my cat."

"At least they let you off with a warning," Kinney said. "It could have been worse. If you can't figure out how

Roberto is escaping the house, you need to lock him in a room when you're out. For his own safety."

"He thinks he's helping." There was a pause as Kinney turned to stare at her. "I know how that sounds, which proves I haven't completely gone off the deep end, right?"

Kinney laughed. "Well, you wouldn't be the first person in Dog Town to over-identify with a pet. I used to think my dog could read my mind."

"She probably could. I never gave as much credit to cats, but I swear he does understand me."

Starting the car again, Kinney said, "Let's keep him alive then, shall we? From now on, you leave this in my hands."

"Are you going to share it with the CCD?"

"Not yet. Like you, I've got some in-house problems. A dirty dog cop barely got spanked for setting up Sasha Wildwood's grooming shop. He should have been drummed out of town." She pulled into Evie's driveway. "I'll start poking around very carefully. We'll find this deadbeat and keep it quiet. For the good of the public and those poor animals."

Evie let out a long sigh. "You have no idea how much of a relief it is to share this."

"Trust me, I do," Kinney said. "Sometimes I'm so full of this town's secrets I feel like I'm choking."

A familiar thump made Kinney jump. But not Evie. Not this time. The orange face staring in at them through the windshield barely startled her at all. That was more of a surprise than the cat itself. "Kinney, meet Roberto the Red," she said.

Kinney leaned forward until her nose practically touched the glass. On the other side, Roberto brushed his face against the windshield, first one cheek, and then the other.

"Get him in here," Kinney said. "We're taking a ride."

"What? Why?"

"He's got a tracking device on his collar. Someone wants to know where Roberto hangs out. So let's give them a run for their money."

CHAPTER EIGHTEEN

Clarence Dayton's home sat on the edge of a ravine, so far back from the road that Evie felt a little nervous going alone. She'd expected something derelict, maybe even creepy, but the house was trim and bright, with dozens of tulips and daffodils nodding a cheery greeting as she walked up the front stairs.

When the door opened, the good cheer evaporated. Clarence's grizzled hair and beard were definitely less well kept than his gardens, and his eyes were dull and dark behind round spectacles.

"Not interested," he said, starting to close the door.

"I'm not selling anything," Evie said, offering her best public relations smile.

"First, everyone's selling something. And second, with that smile, you're selling hard. And I'm not buying."

He kept the door open a crack, so she forged on. "Mr. Dayton, I'm sorry to barge in on you like this. My name is Evelyn Springdale and I'm—"

"Living in Bill Bradshaw's back pocket," he interrupted. "The air must get pretty ripe sometimes. Unless his so-called spiritual enlightenment has him blowing rainbow bubbles instead of stale old farts."

Evie tried to hold back a snort and failed. "I'm sorry," she said. "Allergies."

Clarence cracked the door open a little more, intrigued. "What's a nice girl with a sense of humor doing in a place like that?"

She put her purse down between her feet and crossed her arms. "Honestly, I don't really know how I ended up here. Of all places. I barely like animals, you know." She covered her mouth and muttered, "Blasphemy."

The door opened all the way. "Come in. I'm still not buying, but I'll listen."

The interior of the house was as neat as the exterior. Spring flowers filled half a dozen vases in the vast living room, which was filled with dated furniture still in good shape. The dining room—also large—was empty.

"Not one for entertaining?" she asked, as they passed through to the kitchen at the back of the house.

"The dining set is out for repair," he said. "But no. Basically I detest most people. Especially Dog Town people."

"And yet you're still here," Evie said, settling on an upholstered chair at the table. The fabric and the wood frame had deep scratches from cats, dogs, or both. "You could be anywhere but you're in Dorset Hills."

"You missed the point," he said, sitting opposite and folding his hands on the table. "I said I hate Dog Towners. I love Dorset Hills. Or at least the Dorset Hills of my memory... before it turned into this circus."

"Speaking of circuses," Evie began. "I heard your grandfather took in animals retired from circuses across the country."

"Retired?" Clarence frowned. "They were abandoned,

abused, and about to be shot. He gave them a home, no matter how far gone they were."

"At the Dayton Manor," she said.

"When it was just our family home." His eyes sharpened. "Why are you here, exactly?"

"The Easter festival," she said. "We're set to hold it on the grounds of your grandfather's estate. When I heard you were still—"

"Kicking?"

"—living in town, I decided to ask you to be the guest of honor at the event."

There was a small screech as Clarence pushed his chair away from the table. "Never. I will not step foot on the grounds."

"Why not?" Evie was perplexed. She hadn't had time to dig around much. Remi had mentioned Clarence in passing and she'd decided on a whim to drop in on her way home from work. The house wasn't far from Ruth Banks', and likely within the radius Roberto could walk carrying a rescued animal. "It's your family home."

"*Was* my family home. My mother bequeathed it to the city when I was travelling the world. Or so they say." He knitted his pale fingers together. "She was ill. I don't believe she'd have done that in her right mind, but no one would admit otherwise. I couldn't be bothered with a legal battle. Doesn't mean I'm not still angry."

"Of course. The mansion is worth many millions."

"It's not that. I have enough." He gestured to the window and the expansive yard and gardens that merged with thick brush into the ravine. "It's about the hypocrisy. They made us out to be crazy even when I was a boy. No one talks about how they took my grandfather's rescues away. Town Council said they were a public safety risk after Trickster got into the neighbor's yard and ate her apple tree."

"Trickster was a horse?"

"An elephant," Clarence said. "With a sweet tooth. Crushing that tree is the only damage she ever did. I was only seven when a team of 10 men came to take her away. I can still hear her terrible screech as they drove away. She was that attached to my granddad."

Evie's hand went to her throat. "I'm so sorry. The poor thing."

"Grandfather was never the same after that. They took his big cats and his monkeys, too, but nothing hurt as much as Trickster." He got up and stared out the back window. "So, no, I will not support your event or this city. Dorset Hills is going down the same path now as they did then. Banning chickens, and even cats. It's ridiculous."

Evie agreed with him, so she didn't say anything.

Eventually he went to the door and opened it. A calico cat ran in and looped between his feet in a tight figure eight.

"This is Ramona," he said. "One of my lovely outdoor cats who's at risk of Bill Bradshaw's wrath."

"She's a beauty," Evie said, as Ramona came over and began weaving the same figure eight between her feet. She had thought the move was unique to Roberto, but perhaps it was a standard cat maneuver.

"I won't be chased out of Dorset Hills," Clarence said. "My history is here. It's in my bones."

"I understand and I don't blame you." She cleared her throat. "But since you've mentioned bones... Do you know if any of your grandad's rescues were buried on the estate?"

"Of course. No one thought anything of that back then." Clarence smirked. "Wait till you see the gardens in full bloom. They're spectacular. And they're deeply rooted in a past Dog Town doesn't want to acknowledge." He sat down again. "I won't lie: that makes me happy."

Now Evie was the one to shudder, as she thought of the bag of bones in her brother's shed. Jon had sent some of them away to be tested, but chose a lab out of state for anonymity.

"I'd love to see your gardens," she said, gesturing to the window.

Clarence nodded and got up again. But then he seemed to think better of it. "You seem like a nice young lady. Too nice to get chewed up in the Dog Town gristmill. But I don't want to spend a second more thinking about Bill Bradshaw's regime than I have to. I'm sorry."

Evie rose and touched his arm lightly. "Don't be. I know exactly how you feel."

He walked her out to her car. "You're easier to handle than the small one," he said. "I can only take her in doses."

"The small one?"

"Cori's her name. She comes by now and then to check on me." He gave Evie a tired smile. "She wants something, too, but I haven't figured out what it is."

"She's a puzzle wrapped in an enigma," Evie said. "But I promise you she's not sharing space with me in Bill Bradshaw's back pocket."

A gleeful expression crossed Clarence's face. "I'd love to see what Cori would do with that real estate. Bill would never sit comfortably again."

Evie laughed as she slid into the car. "If you change your mind, let me know. The Bill Bradshaws of the world don't last forever."

"True, but each politician's more corrupt than the last, I've found. You must have a thick hide, young lady."

"I've got something better," she said. "Nine lives."

He slapped the hood of the car as she closed the door and rolled down the window. "Guard them carefully."

SETTLING INTO HER COMFORTABLE ARMCHAIR, Evie patted her lap. Roberto didn't play hard to get. He landed lightly, turned twice and collapsed on his side. His purr was rough, like a motor turning over, but it smoothed out as it got going.

"You're tired, too?" She smothered a sneeze in her shoulder as she stroked the creamy mango-colored fur under his chin. His ears went back. "What? If I'm disrupting your peace with my sneezing, maybe you could try not shedding."

She groped for the remote in the cushions and then saw it lying on the coffee table. The trouble with cats was that once they got themselves artfully arranged, you hated unsettling them. Maybe it was just as well that she couldn't watch TV, as she'd surely doze off. The past eight days had been more exhausting than the last eight jobs put together.

Well, almost.

"I don't think Clarence is the one," she told the cat. "I mean, he *could* be. He's descended from eccentric rescuers who like exotic animals, and he has a longstanding beef with the city. But he loves cats, and I'm starting to think that makes people redeemable. I didn't see any suspicious signs, and he's... well, he's likeable." Roberto flexed his claws ever-so-slightly into her leg, as if to keep her sharp. "Ow! I know, I know, appearances can be deceiving. I guess I'd prefer the villain of this tale to be Leann Cosgrove. And not just to get her off my back professionally."

Roberto' eyes were half-closed, the green barely showing. His sides rose and fell, rose and fell, and the purring seemed to cast a spell over her. Her own eyelids drooped and she fought to stay awake, to keep thinking. This mystery wasn't going to solve itself.

"Maybe a little rest wouldn't hurt," she murmured. "My brain might work better."

The cat's purr grew louder and louder as her thoughts receded, and she imagined herself flying over Dorset Hills on a sunny evening. Her lips twitched into a smile. The rolling hills were spectacular and City Hall, as she swooped over it, looked quaint and benign. Picking off the bronze statues one by one in her dream, she soared toward home, circling briefly over the ravine and Clarence's house. A tiny red sports car two doors down caught her eye. It was no bigger than a toy. Once, twice, three times she circled, floating like a hawk in the updraft. Why hadn't she realized how beautiful this city was? She hadn't been paying enough attention.

Twenty claws brought her fully awake in an instant. Roberto took off from her lap and careened into the kitchen, where he knocked over his stainless-steel bowls with a clatter. She got up from the chair and followed, shaking her head to dispel the aerial image of her neighborhood. There was something she was missing, and her unconscious seemed determined to make her figure it out.

"What's wrong?" she said, as Roberto raced out of the kitchen again and disappeared up the stairs. Something had spooked him, but she couldn't see what. Shrugging, she muttered, "Silly cat. Might as well go to bed, then." It was barely nine p.m., according to the big clock over the table, but tomorrow would doubtless be another trying day of political wrangling.

After wiping up spilled water, she put the cat bowls

in the dishwasher. He preferred drinking directly from the leaky faucet anyway. Then she turned out the lights and headed for the stairs. Just as she passed the front door, she saw a shape move into the rectangular foggy glass window of the door. A tall man, whose outstretched hand looked like a claw. A scream slipped out as the door-bell rang.

"Evie? You okay?" A familiar voice... but whose? "*Evie!*"

Hands still trembling, she touched the doorknob and its smooth, cool surface grounded her. "Who is it?"

"It's Zeke Mackey." A long pause. "Your boss?"

Blowing out a shaky sigh, she twisted the knob and pulled until Zeke's face appeared. His dark hair was ruffled from a brisk wind and his hands were deep in the pockets of his leather jacket. "What was that about?"

"I fell asleep for a few minutes. Something startled me awake and I guess I got spooked." She forced a smile. "I'm sorry. That wasn't a pleasant greeting."

"It's okay. You had me worried for a sec. I thought I might have to break the glass."

"No such heroics necessary, but thank you." She paused, waiting for him to speak, and when he didn't, continued. "What's up? Did something happen at work?"

"Something's always happening at work, isn't it?" He pulled a hand out of his pocket and ran it through his hair. "May I come in?"

The question reminded her of the vampires in one of the TV series she loved. Needing permission to cross the threshold. Well. All political staff were vampires in one way or another... including her.

"Sure. But now I'm concerned. What can't wait till morning?"

"You worry too much. Nick was right." He followed her

into the kitchen. "I just wanted to make sure you're settling in okay, since he's not around to check in on you."

"I'm totally fine. Do you want a cup of tea?"

"If that's all you're offering." He gave her a mischievous smile as he pulled out a chair and sat down. His long legs seemed to dwarf her furniture.

"It's all I've got," she said. "Like you said, I'm still settling in."

"Tea it is." He stared around the kitchen. "Place could use some work."

Plugging in the kettle, she nodded. "Rental. We'll see how it goes. As you know, I tend to move around a lot."

"Dog Town's different. You'll want to stay. I can't tell you how many times I've tried to move and it's like my foot's cuffed to a bronze statue."

"Everyone seems to feel that way," she said, laughing. "Although they're not so eloquent."

"I'd have more opportunity in a bigger city, but I grew up here and it's hard to imagine starting over somewhere... normal." He crooked one long leg over the other, and it struck her how far his good looks and smooth style could take him elsewhere. "I'm very loyal to Bill, however. Maybe when he retires, I can try something new."

"I'm curious about the yoga and meditation," she said, reaching for the teapot and a couple of mugs. "It doesn't seem to fit with what I'd learned about him."

"Surprised me, too. He took quite a beating politically for a few months, so I guess he's trying to find a new balance. There are worse ways than yoga."

"Definitely." Unplugging the kettle, she poured hot water over the teabags in the pot. "But how deep does it go? He's not exactly forging a new peace with dog breeders.

Honestly, Zeke, there's got to be a better way to handle that."

"We're handling it. Don't you worry."

"I don't know. Seems like every time something comes up, you and the mayor are out of the office."

"That's because we're handling it somewhere else." He shrugged. "Isn't it flattering that we know you can hold the fort?"

"I guess. But I'd rather be part of the discussion."

He flicked his fingers to shoo the conversation away. "Let's talk it all out with the mayor in the morning. Tonight's mission was meant to be personal. You look tired, if you don't mind my saying."

"Really, I'm fine." She set a mug in front of him, collected milk from the fridge and sat down across from him. "Getting shouted down by protestors takes it out of you, of course. I'll rest easier after we chat with the mayor."

A flicker of what seemed like impatience crossed his handsome features, as she resisted his attempt to steer the conversation into a different lane. Could Nick have been right about Zeke being interested? If so, she'd have to nip that in the bud very delicately.

"It must be hard to be on your own in a new town," he tried again. "I'm sure you came expecting to spend time with Nick. You need to get out into the hills for some fresh air. Watch the dogs play."

She stirred her tea and sipped before answering. "I'd be too worried about getting ambushed by angry dog breeders. There are so many of them."

"Well, you'd need company, of course. Someone who's known the trails all his life."

And... there it was... Now for the fancy footwork. "That does sound like fun. But I'm an all-work, no-play kind of girl. So until things are on an even keel at City Hall, I'll keep a low profile."

If he noticed the slight he didn't let on. Instead, he tipped the last of his tea down his throat and said, "You could just trust me that things have a way of working themselves out around here. What you resist persists, and what you embrace—"

"Dissolves," she finished. "Don't let my brother hear you talk that way, Zeke. He'll laugh you out of town."

"Let him try," he said, grinning. "I'm not going anywhere, and neither are you. I know you have hopes for making a difference here. You said something to Hannah Pemberton about a service dog center of excellence."

"Yes!" The idea hadn't come out quite so well formed, but she liked it.

"Why don't you put a proposal together? We can hash things out when the dust settles on the new regulations."

In other words, never. The dust around these regulations was radioactive.

"Don't look so skeptical," he said. "I already spoke to the mayor and he said the idea aligned with his new platform of peace."

"Okay, I'll put something together." She tried to sound cool, but her heart, ever-hopeful, had started turning cartwheels. This was what she was in Dorset Hills to do, she was sure of it. It would all fall into place once she sorted out the breeders and disbanded the exotic pet ring.

"How's it going with the Rescue Mafia?" he asked. "Keeping a finger on the pulse?"

"Working on it. They're definitely interested in the service dog project."

"Good," he said, getting up. "Keep your enemies close, and your friends distant."

"An interesting twist on an old saying," she said, walking behind him to the front door. His head swivelled as he took the place in. If he was trying to get a fix on her, there wasn't much to go on. Thank goodness he hadn't visited a few days earlier, when there was a capybara bleating in the bathtub. Even the cat bowls had disappeared, thanks to Roberto's earlier clatter.

After seeing Zeke out, she went upstairs and changed into her pajamas. There was no sign of the cat, but 20 itchy red pinpricks on her thighs made her briefly homesick for San Francisco, when all she had to worry about was regular politics.

Roberto sauntered into the room, jumped onto her bed and curled up on her pillow. "Off," she said, tipping him sideways and flipping the pillow. "I've had enough of pushy males for one night."

CHAPTER NINETEEN

In the morning, Evie showered and took a little extra care with her hair and makeup. She tried on three different outfits, wondering what would make just the right impression on the enlightened mayor, paving the way to the service dog center of excellence. In the end, she settled on her favorite knit dress and heels. It felt like a big hug, and she needed that today.

"What you resist persists," she told Roberto as she followed him downstairs. "Did you know that? And what you embrace dissolves. Be one with what is, whatever that is."

He offered a purr-meow that had more to do with reminding her about his breakfast. She got a bowl out of the cupboard and emptied a tin of revolting-smelling food into the bowl as she caught his eye.

"Look. I'm sorry to tell you this, but you're going to have to spend the day upstairs. I want you to be safe so I'm going to put you in the spare room. Don't worry. I'll bring up the litter box, and make sure I'm home on time. You need to catch up on your beauty sleep anyway."

He wove around her feet, and she set down the food. "Glad you're taking it so well, buddy."

Once she had him fed and settled upstairs, she grabbed her coat and opened the front door. Her jaw dropped and her eyes widened. Outside, at least 30 people had formed a picket line blocking her driveway. They were carrying placards, and when they saw the door open, they erupted into shouts. "*Back off breeders. Back off breeders.*"

She slipped back into the house, slammed the door and pulled out her phone. After a quick text to Zeke she steeled herself to go out again. Her hands shook but her jaw set. She would not remain a prisoner in her own home. If she couldn't get the car out of the driveway, she'd sneak out the back door, climb the fence and go through the yards until she got to a side street. Now her outfit felt less like a hug and more like an accident waiting to happen. "It'll be fine," she called to Roberto. "Stay calm."

Hand on the doorknob, she took three long breaths from the diaphragm, and felt her heart rate slow. The mayor was really onto something with this yoga breathing. Opening the door again, she plastered on a bright smile. The chanting started again and she waved.

"Good morning, everyone! You guys have more energy than I have—at least without my coffee. How about we all head down to City Hall, get caffeinated, and chat about the new regulations. I think it's time we called in the big guns." The breeders took a collective step back. "The mayor, I mean. I've heard your concerns and it's time he did, too."

A new chant began. "No more talk. No more talk."

"Talk's what I've got," she said. "I can't do much more with people holding me hostage in my own home. Is that how you do things in Dog Town?"

"If you have to ask, you don't belong here," Leann's

voice rang out. She was standing in the middle of the lineup, wearing her usual black and blue lumberjacket. "Go home. Go home. Go home."

The line advanced onto her property and her heart rate picked up again. She had wanted Dorset Hills to become home, but that was starting to look impossible. Tears pricked in her eyes and she blinked rapidly. First rule of PR: never let them see you cry or sweat.

She reached behind to let herself back into the house. Time for Plan B.

Just then came a blaring honk. The car sounded bigger than a Prius. The driver's window rolled down and a voice boomed out over a speaker. "Disband immediately. The police are on their way. If you step foot in Bellington Square today, you face a significant fine."

Leann tossed Kinney a string of profanity, and she didn't need a megaphone to be heard.

"Furthermore," Kinney boomed, "I have the CCD's permission to spot check the property of any breeder in the city today. If I discover a single dog hair out of place, there will be consequences. So I ask you... do you have time to picket, or is there some cleanup to do at home?"

It was like spraying hot water on ice. The crowd dissolved without so much as another word, even from Leann, although she made some hand gestures reminiscent of Cori's.

Kinney pulled into Evie's driveway and hopped out. "You okay?"

Coming down the front stairs, Evie said, "I've been better, actually."

"No kidding. Get in the car and I'll drop you at City Hall."

When she got settled in the passenger seat, Evie turned. "I'm so glad Zeke sent you."

Kinney's eyebrows twitched but she kept her eyes on the road. Some of the protestors deliberately blocked their path and she rolled down the window again. "Making a list, checking it twice," she called. "Guess who's on the naughty list?"

The breeders stepped out of the way, but one slapped the Prius as it eased past.

Finally Kinney spoke. "Zeke didn't send me... Cori did."

"Cori Hogan?"

"The same. She got wind of the protest and texted early." Reaching for her phone, she took a look. "Nothing from Zeke."

Evie checked her own phone. "Seriously? His whole 'I'm worried about you' visit last night was a crock of crap."

"He visited you last night?"

"Weird, right? He said he was watching over me for my brother, but where is he now?"

Kinney pressed the pedal down and the statues flew past. "Seems like Zeke and the mayor are only watching over their own butts. Guess who's watching over yours?"

"Cori, evidently. But how do you know she wasn't in on it somehow?"

Turning into the City Hall parking lot, Kinney said, "Because I've known her for 10 years. She's a pain in the arse—everyone's arse—but she won't participate in stupid pack behavior."

Evie got out of the car, then leaned back in. "Thank you. And I'll thank Cori when I see her. For now, I've got a bone to pick with my bosses."

"Metaphorically, I hope," Kinney said. "Leave the real bones alone."

Evie flew upstairs, in a flurry of indignation. Ignoring Chloe, she tossed her coat on a chair in the reception area, rapped on the mayor's door and then opened it. He was sitting behind his massive oak desk, with his head tipped back against the leather chair. She thought for one chilling moment that he was dead, but when she gasped his eyes opened.

"Evelyn, don't you knock? I was meditating."

"I did knock, sir."

His expression softened. "Ah. Well I must be getting better at this, then, because I didn't even hear it."

"I'm sorry to bother you, but there was an incident this morning. I came out my front door to find dozens of dog breeders picketing. They had me trapped."

"Oh, is that what Zeke was fussing about? He was trying to get my attention but I've blocked off 8 to 9 for mindfulness. No exceptions." He checked the clock over her head. "I'll make up 10 minutes later." He gestured to the chair facing his desk and she perched lightly on the edge. "Now, take a few breaths from the diaphragm and tell me about it.

Relieved to have his full attention, she shared all the details of recent meetings, her breeder visits, and the protest in Bellington Square. The mayor rested his elbows on his desk, tented his fingers over his nose and leaned on them. By the time she started on the driveway takeover, his eyes had closed, and she wondered if he was paying off the 10 minutes he owed the universe.

When she stopped talking, however, his eyes opened again. "What I'm hearing is that this has been really annoying for you."

"Well, yes sir. It's an invasion of privacy. At least a third of those protestors were men, and now they know where I live."

"Evelyn, be calm. Remember, what you resist persists, and—"

"What you embrace dissolves. I do remember, sir, but I won't be embracing any irate protestors at my home."

"Would you feel safer at a hotel? We could put you up until things settle."

A beatific smile settled over his handsome features. It was eerie. He seemed like a different man than the one she'd seen in interviews—even the man she'd met less than two weeks ago. She knew many people on spiritual journeys in San Francisco, and none had experienced such rapid transformation.

"The protestors would find me there in no time, and they could trash my house before they came looking. What I'd really like is to get this issue sorted out." She leaned forward. "If I may speak frankly—"

"I'd rather you didn't. Stress is the enemy of the spirit, Evelyn." He pushed his chair back. "Anyway, I got the picture."

"I just wanted to say that I feel like this office has... has thrown me to the dogs, sir." He started to speak and she held up her hand. "Yes, my job is PR. Yes, I'm used to dealing with irate stakeholders. What I'm not used to is senior officials avoiding me and dismissing my recommendations. There are ways to bring order to the dog breeding community without raising so much ire. Some of these people actually share your concerns and want more regulation."

"Breathing, Evelyn, breathing... It's all going to work out just fine. Zeke has assured me of that." He crossed his legs and flashed some teeth. "I left it all in his capable hands and he has a plan."

"If he does, he hasn't shared it. It looks like he's hoping their infighting leaves them too disorganized to lobby effectively."

The mayor shrugged. "There are worse strategies."

"There are better ones, too. Strategies that would build up morale in important Dog Town citizens."

"They're not as important as they like to think they are." He sighed and closed his eyes again. "None of us is. At any rate, I don't want to be troubled by all of this. I hired Zeke, and then you, to take care of these things. I'm under doctor's orders to reduce stress. Just having you flutter around in here like a trapped moth is raising my blood pressure."

"Well, I'm sorry about that, sir. If it weren't a matter of personal safety…"

"Just book a hotel and lie low for a bit," the mayor said. "This will blow over."

She made a circuit of the office, and then remembered his trapped moth comment. "I wasn't expecting this, Mayor."

"I understand, Evelyn." His smile returned. "Things are probably quite different in big city politics. You'll get used to this."

She would not get used to it, she was quite sure of that. "But—"

"One moment…" The mayor tinkered with his phone.

The door burst open and Zeke strode into the room. "Evie, I'm so sorry. I just got your text. I was out for a run. I see that all's well. Did you call the police?"

"No, I didn't call the police."

"Well, you should have. These people deserve to get their butts hauled in." He turned to the mayor. "I'm sorry we intruded on your quiet time, Mayor. Luckily, Evie broke it up before the media arrived. Mind you, a neighbor did post one photo online, which I asked them to take down." He nodded to the mayor's computer. "I emailed it to you."

The mayor turned and switched it on, all without urgency. One click brought up a photo of the disturbance in front of Evie's home.

"Well, that is quite a crowd, isn't it?" the mayor said. "It's a shame. They don't realize the importance of morning mental hygiene. Now their whole day is off kilter."

"Look at the roof, sir," Zeke said. "By the chimney. Blow up the image."

The mayor did just that, and then reared back. "Evelyn, what's this?"

She leaned in. Sitting on the ridge of the roof in the chimney's shadow was Roberto. His tail was wrapped neatly around his paws and his green eyes seemed to issue a challenge.

"It appears to be an orange tabby cat," she said.

"You told me you don't have any pets, and that you don't like cats."

"Just because he's sitting on my roof doesn't mean I own him."

Zeke spoke up. "The neighbor says he's in and out of your place all the time."

"Evelyn, I'm disappointed," the mayor said. "You lied at our first meeting."

"I didn't lie." She paced back and forth in front of his desk, and then stopped. "That cat was outside my house the night of our meeting. He was injured and I decided to help him recover."

"He looks in perfect health. I guess he doesn't know the City doesn't support cats being outdoors."

"He does know, actually."

The mayor crooked his eyebrow. "Really?"

She crooked her eyebrow back. "Well, I've told him so, but he's an escape artist."

"Then I suggest you surrender him before you move to the hotel," the mayor said. "Zeke, if you don't mind…"

Zeke circled behind Evie, and without actually touching her, started to push her out of the office.

Evie stopped at the door. "Thank you for your concern. I will not be moving to a hotel and I won't be giving up the cat, either. I'll take my chances at being attacked by protestors in my own home." She mimicked the mayor's radiant smile. "If something happened to me, I guess it would destroy any public support the dog breeders have. So I can see why you'd be okay with that."

The mayor's eyes became sharp for a moment. "Evelyn, cynicism like that will eat you up from the inside out. Anger only hurts the person experiencing it."

She shrugged. "I'm used to being the political scapegoat, sir."

The mayor gave a feeble wave. "Zeke, please. The atmosphere is getting toxic in here. I won't have it."

Zeke's air pushing turned into real pulling, and the old oak door actually hit her on the way out.

CHAPTER TWENTY

"Well then," Kinney said, pulling out of her parking space beside City Hall. "I guess we just need to stand by and see if the grenade explodes, or just rolls around the mayor's office."

"Zeke told me not to worry," Evie said, rolling down the window to catch a breeze. "But I have a feeling my tenth life starts tomorrow."

"Don't be so quick to call a time of death," Kinney said, turning right instead of left at the exit. "Your ninth life is still hanging by a thread. Let's see if we can resuscitate it."

"Where are we going?" She could barely summon the energy to sound interested. After the altercation with the mayor, Zeke had kept her busy meeting spokespeople for different breed groups. Today it had been the Lab, pumi, border collie, shar-pei and wheaten terrier reps. Tomorrow, 10 more would arrive. And another 10 the day after that. She was to woo them one by one, and prepare a report at the end of her consultation. He'd agreed she could stay in her home, however, and asked the police to patrol periodically to keep an eye on the place.

"Just enjoy the ride," Kinney said, smiling.

"If it involves alcohol, I'm all for it."

"Get through all this and we'll throw a party." Keeping her left hand on the wheel, she patted Evie's arm with her right. "Why don't you just chill for 10 minutes?"

"I'm not going to meditate, if that's what you're suggesting. If I never hear the word 'mindfulness' again, it will be too soon."

Just the same, she subsided into silence and stared out the window. Kinney cruised along until they passed one of the Lab bronzes standing sentry on the city, and then she sped up. Evie pressed her forehead against the glass, watching dusk fall over the city. You could see people in their homes cooking dinner and playing with their kids and dogs. It looked like domestic bliss, something that evidently wasn't in the cards for her.

"It's not that bad," Kinney said. "I've seen worse situations turn out great. Just you wait."

"Okay," she said. "And thank you for going to my place and putting Roberto inside. I had him locked in the spare room this morning, I promise."

"I guess you didn't notice the opening to the attic over the built-in wardrobe. That shameless feline tried to repeat the move right in front of me. So, he can stay in the bathroom, where the only way out is down the drain."

"I wouldn't put it past him," Evie said, smiling in spite of herself. "He looked so cocky sitting up on that roof that I had to claim him. Whatever happens, Roberto's coming with me. Who cares if my nose is red for the rest of his life?"

"It's the right choice," Kinney said, pulling into a gravel driveway. There was a large city sign at the entrance but it was behind them before Evie had time to read it. Kinney confidently bumped over the rough terrain as if she'd been here before. At the end of the parking lot she pulled up beside an old lime-green van. "They're already here."

"Who? And more importantly, did they bring tequila?"

Kinney laughed as she got out of the car and a voice instantly shushed her. Up ahead, a flashlight bobbed in the dim light. They followed, turning on the lights of their phones.

"Stay behind me," Kinney said. "And watch the trail. You'll need to be super careful in those shoes."

"You could have mentioned we were going hiking," Evie muttered. This was the last straw for her footwear collection. Heels might be part of her armor in the office, but they were a hazard everywhere else.

"I only found out half an hour ago," she said.

There was a sound of disgust ahead. "What part of 'quiet' didn't you understand?"

Kinney snorted. "The part where there's no one around for miles."

"The walls have ears. Even where there are no walls," the voice said.

"Cori Hogan," Evie whispered.

Another hiss for silence. "Did you have to bring her?" Cori said.

"It's about her," Kinney said. "So, yes."

Her voice was closer, because the people ahead had stopped in a clearing. Evie scanned with her light and saw Cori standing in front of Bridget Linsmore and Andrea MacDuff. Nika Lothian and Maisie Todd were sitting at the base of a bronze statue. Even with individual circles of light pooling, it wasn't possible to identify the statue's breed. It looked fluffy, if brass could be fluffy.

"Hey, Evie," Bridget said. "Nice to see you again."

"You too. Looks like I've crashed your mafia meeting."

"That's true," Cori said. "Some people don't take our privacy very seriously." She crossed her arms, glaring.

The evening was balmy and heavy with the scent of spring, but Cori still wore her black wool gloves with the neon orange middle fingers. Evie wondered if there was a summer version in cotton.

"Thanks for meeting us," Kinney said, undaunted. "Evie's had a rough day."

"Oh boo-hoo for the political advisor," Cori said. "You can't expect us to feel sorry for you."

"I don't, actually," Evie said. "Thank you for tipping Kinney off about the protest this morning."

Cori shot Kinney a look. "You told her?"

Kinney shrugged. "I had to. She was giving credit to the chief of staff."

"Who threw her under the bus," Cori said, shaking her head.

"Looks like it," Evie said. "But they're keeping me around to make sure they get the most use out of me. And I want to stick around long enough to solve a little mystery."

"Oh?" Cori's brown eyes met hers and they glinted in the flashlight's glow. "Do tell."

Evie gestured to Kinney, who told the story of Roberto and the exotic animals. The women were mostly impassive, as if they'd heard too many crazy stories before. But when Kinney got to the Burmese python, everyone except Cori flinched. When she described the bag of bones, however, Cori was the first to flinch. Then she wedged herself between Nika and Maisie on the base of the statue.

"We need your help," Kinney said. "I've been digging but I haven't turned up anything, and I don't really want to draw in the rest of the CCD."

"Because it's a nest of vipers," Cori said. "Like we

warned you when you went over to the dark side. Now you're trying to get things done within the system."

Kinney rolled her eyes, as if she'd heard that whine before. "It's not such a bad thing to have someone inside and others outside. For example, I checked with the utility companies to see if there were any houses using more fuel than expected."

Cori looked moderately impressed. "And were there?"

"Too many to be indicative, actually. It's like everyone's got a grow op in Riverdale."

"What else have you tried?" Bridget asked.

"I've got a list of known dog breeders in the area, and I'm comparing it to police reports and neighbor complaints. Our theory is that a dog breeder is more likely to be able to care for exotics."

"Plus they're disgruntled," Evie added. "It's a way to thumb their nose at the City and make up for a potential loss in income."

"Possibly," Duff said. "But sometimes there's no good reason for these things. Maybe someone just likes snakes and saw a business opportunity."

"I've got someone monitoring all buy-and-sell sites for exotics," Kinney said. "That will probably pay out but it could take a while. Plus I put the tracking device from the cat in an abandoned garage with a camera on it in case someone collects."

"In the meantime, there's a capybara that needs to go home to mom," Bridget said. "How's he doing?"

"It's a she," Evie said. "Letitia."

Cori offered another disgusted sound. "The dog-hater is naming the exotics. Next thing we'll see her carrying the capybara around in a snuggly. She's as bad as Remi and that beagle."

"Don't badmouth Remi," Duff said. "She's one of us."

"If she were one of us she'd be here," Cori said. "*You're* barely one of us. And Kinney is no longer one of us."

Bridget turned toward Cori and it was like the air leaked out of the smaller woman. "We're grateful to anyone who helps us in our cause," she said. "Especially Kinney, who's risking her job."

To break the tension, Evie said, "The capybara is doing surprisingly well. She's in a safe house now because she's so darn noisy."

"You've done well handling all this as a pet and rescue novice," Bridget said. "Kudos."

"Not with much confidence," Evie said. "But I'm getting over my fear faster than I would have thought. I'm very fond of the cat and quite like three dogs. The snake... not so much."

"That's a big change for a couple of weeks," Cori said, skeptically.

Kinney stepped forward. "She defended her cat with the mayor today. A neighbor got a shot of him on the roof during the protest."

"Huh. Well, that's something." Cori's voice warmed a few degrees. "What do you need us for, Kinney?"

"You're going to make me ask?" Kinney said.

For the first time that night, Cori grinned. "Yeah. I'd really like to hear it."

"I need you to do your thing. Work your magic to help us rescue these exotic pets before another one turns up dead in the Dayton Manor garden."

Cori cracked her knuckles under her gloves. "Bring it on."

"I'm worried about the Easter festival," Evie added. "I'd

hate to have a dog turn up another skull and terrify the kids."

"It'll be fine," Cori said. "All you need is a higher value prize and the dogs won't even look for the bones."

"And that is...?"

"Meet me at Monster Zoo at 10 tomorrow morning and I'll give you a free consultation."

Something told Evie that nothing was ever free with Cori, but she simply said, "Thank you, Cori. I appreciate it."

Getting up, Cori led the crew back down the trail. "Just follow my lead without question, understood? Keep quiet and you might actually learn something about managing people."

CHAPTER TWENTY-ONE

Monster Zoo was the biggest pet supplies store in the greater Dorset Hills area. There were countless cute and quirky boutiques within the city, but serious dog owners usually headed out to the Wychwood Grove suburb to stock up at Monster Zoo, where you could literally back up to the loading bay and have your kibble dropped into the trunk.

Evie wasn't surprised Cori preferred Monster Zoo to the boutiques. She looked comfortable roaming the rows of toys, picking up one after the other and rolling her eyes. "Nearly all of them brag about being indestructible, but most could be easily ripped apart and ingested by a motivated dog. It keeps the vets in business, fishing toys out of dog guts."

"So, how do we find a toy safe enough to hold a treat without destroying it?"

"We don't. We find the best option possible, warn the owners to be vigilant and keep a vet on standby. Your boyfriend will do."

"He's not my boyfriend," Evie said, flushing. "I've only known him two weeks."

Cori picked up a small red plastic block and shook her head. "Newsflash: if he's hiding your capybara and kinkajou, he's your boyfriend."

Evie offered her a rubber food dispensing ball. "So now you're an expert on romance?"

"Hardly. Bridget's the matchmaker." She put the rubber ball back. "I'm just an observer of human and canine behavior."

"Why don't we ask for help? It will take us all day to go through these toys."

"I know what I'm looking for," she said, glancing over her shoulder. "And there she is now."

Striding toward them was Leann Cosgrove, in her usual lumberjacket and work boots. She wasn't a particularly large woman, but she certainly knew how to claim a space. Her shoulders were back, her head high, and her brown eyes as sharp as Cori's. When she saw Evie, she did a double take, lurched to a stop, and then turned.

"You're here now, Leann," Cori said. "Might as well help us out."

"Why would I help *her* out?" She gestured with a thumb toward Evie, refusing to look at her.

"Think of it this way," Cori said. "You're not helping Evie or the City, but the dogs. There will be at least a hundred of them at this Easter Festival sniffing for the treasures we hide. The dog who collects the most gets a ton of prizes, including private training with me."

"No offense, but—"

"What comes after that lead-in is always offensive." Cori grinned at Evie, to give her credit for the line.

"Whatever. It's just more Dog Town stupidity and I want no part of it," Leann said.

"A lot of your clients and mine will come out in full force with dogs you've bred and I've trained. I don't want them to end up in emergency with an obstruction, do you?"

"If it embarrasses the City, then I'm all for it," Leann said.

"Oh please, Leann. There's no way you'd allow *any* dog to be hurt if you could stop it. Who better to know what will work for this than a hound breeder? With their famous noses and appetite, beagles will rock this game. But they're also among the most likely to swallow the prize."

Leann sighed. "Cori, you're the person I most love to hate in this town." She shot Evie a dark look. "Political staff don't qualify as people."

Cori actually laughed at this, and now Evie was the one shooting a dark look. But she remembered Cori's request to follow her lead, so she fell back and let the other two sort through rack after rack of toys. Finally, after close inspection, Leann pronounced, "This is it."

The toy in question was a large, hard plastic egg with small holes in the end, like a pepper shaker. It was so tough to open that they passed it back and forth until Leann finally pried it apart. Then she dropped it on the floor and tried to smash it with her work boot.

"Perfect," Evie said. "Now I need to get 200 and fill them."

"Good luck with that," Leann said, still speaking to Cori. "Am I done here?"

"Here, yes," Cori said, gathering eggs and dropping them into a shopping basket. "Now we head over to your place to test it on your hounds."

"Excuse me?" Evie was surprised Leann could sound so shrill. "I will not have this hack on my property."

"Do you have something to hide?" Cori asked.

"Of course not. The CCD could inspect me any day of the week and find my kennel in good order. I just don't want government cooties anywhere near my impressionable puppies." Her thin lips formed a smile at this. "I've got a litter at home right now."

"Leann, I've always liked your attitude," Cori said. "Most don't. But you might want to spend some time finding the line between your bread and where it's buttered."

"In English, please," Leann said. "Now you're starting to talk bafflegab like a slick politician."

Cori turned and started walking to the checkout. "In plain language? You're playing right into the government's hands with your protests. Breeders are ratting each other out and protesting on private property. Public opinion is turning against you. But it's not too late to get people back on your side."

Walking behind them, Evie saw Leann's shoulders gradually slump as her ego deflated. "How?"

"First, come out to the Easter festival and pitch in. Let people see you smile for a change."

Leann grimaced instead. "What else?"

"Arianna Torrance," Cori said. "She's got the face of an angel and she's smart, too. Put her in front of the mayor and watch him crumble."

"She raises those stupid teddy bears. They're not even a real breed," Leann said.

Cori shrugged. "Everyone's got an opinion. I prefer rescue mutts but teddy bears play well to the public and you might as was well leverage that."

"Since when do you play to the politicians or the public?" Leann asked.

"I play my own game by my own rules," Cori said, gathering eggs from special displays near the checkout. "Rule number one is to put dogs first. All dogs. Smart regulations for all dog breeders will do that."

"Ari can't speak for breeders like me," Leann said. "She's got the money to splash out on a big house and facilities. Most breeders do it for love and barely scrape by."

"Ari's got money because she's a good marketer. Maybe you all could learn something."

"I'll think about what you said," Leann said, turning away.

"Think fast," Cori called after her. "Because Evie's got the lead on a new service dog initiative and it seems to me that beagles are perfect for that role."

Leann stopped and her shoulders straightened again. Her eyes lit on Evie for the first time. "Evie, would you like to test your Easter eggs on my hounds?"

"YOU'RE BRILLIANT," Evie said, as they left Leann's kennel and drove downtown.

"You're not the first to say so." Cori ran one gloved hand through her short hair, leaving static behind. "Oh wait... You are. People frequently miss my brilliance because of my sparkling personality."

Evie laughed, and the sound almost startled her. How long had it been since she'd laughed like that? She felt a little giddy with relief to have Cori and the mafia on her side.

"Well, you'd make an excellent politician," she said. "Would you like my job when I get fired?"

"Thanks, but no thanks." Cori tried to smooth her hair and only made it worse. "You know why my strategy worked so well?"

"Because I kept my mouth shut and followed your lead?"

"Correct. As a result, you witnessed a classic dog training sequence work its magic on a human. First, I made Leann feel respected and liked. Then I offered her a chance to do the right thing, and reinforced the behavior when she did it. When she made a misstep, I gave a quick correction to bring her back in line. And I left her with hope of future rewards."

"No need for a shock collar," Evie said.

"I support corrective devices for humans, but only as a last resort." Cori pulled her car into a parking spot on Main Street and turned off the ignition. "Now we have a supporter, who may bring her followers on board for the benefit of all city dogs."

"Plus you bought me time to snoop around at Leann's when you were testing the toys."

Cori held up her hand for a gloved high five. "Witness my magic."

They got out of the car and wove through the lunchtime crowd on the sidewalk past the Lucky Dog Barkery and The Model Dog, Sasha Wildwood's grooming salon.

"There was no sign of anything more exotic than her American hairless dog. I didn't see that coming, though."

"Leann adopted that rescue from Bridget and me, so she had a home inspection last year. I was pretty sure she was clean." At the older end of Main Street, Cori slowed.

"We've visited a lot of breeders at one point or another, and they're mostly good people."

"Good people don't block someone from leaving her home," Evie said.

Cori opened the door to Bertucci's Fine Italian Meats and they went inside. The store was in the middle of a makeover, but lots of people were taking numbers at the counter.

"Threatened people pack up like scared dogs," she said. "That's what's happening with the breeders. Their businesses often cut so close to the bone that any changes you introduce could prevent them from keeping their dogs." She wagged her index finger, bringing the orange flipper along for the ride. "No good breeder will give up one of her dogs without a huge fight."

"I guess that's what the mayor's counting on. He's been surprisingly sanguine about the whole affair. It's like he's detached. Even stoned."

"I think the stress started getting to him after the Thanksgiving rescue pageant. He'd counted on the TV feature they shot to bring glory to the city but Bridget asked the producer to sit on it for a while. It's like a secret cache of ammunition—something we can hold over the mayor's head."

"Remi says he wasn't the same after Marti Forrester and chicken-gate. It was like his spirit broke, she said."

"I don't believe that," Cori said. "This is a man who was willing to give up his dog for politics. He's just rotten to the core."

"Princess is apparently in a safe house, and he intends to get her back eventually."

Cori had been studying the meat selection, but her head

whipped around. For once she looked surprised. "Really. Why don't I know about this?"

Evie shrugged. "Maybe it wasn't true. But that's what he told me."

"Huh. Well, if it is true—and I'll find out—then it may be possible to rehabilitate him." She took a number and waved to a clerk behind the counter. "I've never given up on a bad dog, you know. If Billy Bradshaw can be salvaged, we just need to move him into a job where he does no harm. And replace him with someone better."

"Cori for mayor," Evie said, grinning.

"There's an idea. I'll let you keep your job. Probably. But some heads would roll."

When their number came up, Cori made her selections of prosciutto, bacon, roast beef and several types of wieners. "This stuff will make any dog hunt," she said. "There's something for every taste. Just make sure there's enough of the eggs around to stop them from fighting."

"I hope this ends well," Evie said, accepting the brown paper packages from the clerk.

"There will be dozens of dog experts on hand to make sure it does," Cori said.

They walked back to the car, and Evie was a little sad their adventure was over. "About that service dog initiative you lied to Leann about... Politicians make a lot of big promises they don't keep."

"Oh, I know that. If it doesn't pan out, it'll be part of a long line of Billy's broken promises. Unless he happens to be salvageable, which, frankly, I doubt."

"Me too. In the meantime, we're no further ahead with Operation Ocelot."

"Sure we are. Before you met me at Monster Zoo, I gave the manager a list of foods for all kinds of exotics and asked him to look into regular buyers. I even asked him to check in-store cameras in the snake food department."

"Good idea. Are you sure he's on the right side?" Evie asked.

"Bridget's dog Beau gave the manager a pass for the pageant, and that dog has spectacular judgement. The store's been a sponsor of the pageant ever since."

"Well I hope he hurries," Evie said. "I've got to get that honey bear out of my brother's house before he gets home or I'll need a safe house, too. Thank goodness he decided to stay in North Carolina an extra week."

Cori pulled something out of her pocket and handed it to her. It was a laser cat toy. "The manager offered me a toy for my dog but I figured you and Roberto could use some fun."

"That's so sweet—"

"Don't bother," Cori interrupted. "As mayor, I'll ban sycophants."

"I can't wait for you to take the throne," Evie said. "We'll need to cut the legs down so you can get on."

"Whoa. Look who thinks she's funny," Cori said, grinning as she flipped her a slice of orange. "Brave too, considering this shorty is standing between you and a hundred dogs crazed by Easter prosciutto."

"Well, that's one way to get over a phobia," Evie said, hailing a cab.

"They call it flooding," Cori said. "You overload the phobic with stimuli and see if she cracks."

Evie hopped into the cab, then called out the window, "What doesn't drown you makes you stronger."

CHAPTER TWENTY-TWO

Roberto had become decidedly clingy. He hated being shut in the bathroom while she was at work, but she figured better safe than roaming. On Good Friday, as she got ready to go out, he turned into a pest—knocking her makeup off the bathroom counter, racing in crazed circles around her bed and over her clothes, and finally, strolling along the kitchen counter when he knew very well it was off limits.

"If you're trying to get my attention, it's working," she said, lifting him down from the counter a second time. "But if you're trying to get me to stay home, no dice. Do you have any idea how long it's been since I've been on a date? Months, that's how long. I barely remember what it's like."

She turned to pour another cup of coffee and he leaped on the counter once more. It was like he was on springs.

"Look, you had quality lap time all morning while I wrote up my stakeholder consultation report. I deserve some fun, don't you think?"

He swatted a spoon off the counter and it clattered to the floor in a spray of cream. She glared at him and he glared back, tail swishing. "You're really annoying. I'm starting to regret my decision to keep you."

She bent over to pick up the spoon and Roberto jumped onto her back. He dug in his claws for balance.

"Hey! Ow! That's my favorite cashmere sweater. Get off, Bert!"

Instead he adjusted position till he was centered between her shoulder blades and pretty much impossible to reach. If she stood up now, he'd either hang there or rip holes in the sweater on his way to the floor. Good things happened in this sweater. She wasn't going to let it go easily.

"You can't keep me prisoner just because you've got itchy feet," she grunted, still stooped over. "One day you'll thank me for keeping you safe."

He had the audacity to lie down between her shoulder blades and start purring. Every so often he flexed his claws to let her know he meant business.

"Roberto. Get off, right now. I mean it. No matter what you do, I am going out for a few hours with Jon. But if you spare my sweater, we'll come back early with Gilda and curl up on the couch together. Doesn't that sound nice?"

The purring stopped and he splayed himself further. It looked like he wasn't going anywhere, so she'd have to choose between risking her sweater and being caught by Jon in this undignified position. The second he arrived on the doorstep, the cat would startle and take off with bits of cashmere stuck in his claws anyway.

She took a few deep breaths to make the cat think she was staying calm. Then she stood upright so suddenly that Roberto fell to the floor with a thud. It was a clumsy landing, completely unlike him, and she immediately felt bad.

"Are you hurt?" She bent over him, and he put his ears

back, gathering himself to jump on her again. "Okay, okay. Forget it."

Keeping her eyes on the cat, she backed carefully out of the kitchen and toward the front door. Roberto followed, trying to work his way around her for another ambush. Their silly little dance continued until Jon's knock. Unlocking the door, she called, "Come in, but be careful. Roberto's in a mood."

Jon slipped into the house without leaving room for an escape artist. When he saw the cat sitting on the back of a living room chair, he let Gilda inside, too. The dog immediately walked over to Roberto and the cat jumped down to greet her, meowing in a tone that sounded like a serious complaint about management. Gilda nudged him as if to assure him all would be well, but he kept pacing.

"He does seem anxious," Jon said. "Did you check his wound?"

"It's fine. Completely healed. I can only assume he doesn't want to be locked in the bathroom while we're out."

"I could leave Gilda here so he has company if you like."

She shook her head. "I don't want her to forfeit the run. Bert will be fine. Maybe I'll put him in the bedroom instead."

They all went upstairs and Jon helped her examine the room from top to bottom to make sure there were no escape routes. She moved the litter box in there, along with bowls of water and kibble.

The cat tried to slip past Jon, but he caught him easily. "I'm an expert at this, mister," he said. "If I can manage a feisty capybara and a mischievous honey bear, I can certainly manage you."

Once the cat was secure, they filed back downstairs. She

paused on the porch after locking the door. "Why do I feel so guilty? I thought cats were supposed to be low maintenance."

"Most are," he said, guiding her down to the van and opening the passenger door. "I've met a lot of quirky cats, but none quite like Roberto."

"Lucky me," she said. "If I ever meet the person who stuck him between my doors, I won't know whether to hug them or slug them."

The rolling hills beckoned, and her spirits rose the further they got from her house. It felt great to forget her worries for a little while. The mayor had been out of the office since their altercation, but Zeke had kept her occupied with a steady stream of meetings and busywork. He was pleasant enough, but she still sensed her days might be numbered. A small cloud swept over her thoughts but she reminded herself she had beautiful scenery, a handsome man and a sweet dog to distract her.

"How are Kinney, Cori and the gang doing with their investigation?" Jon asked.

"No news yet," she said. "I wish I could be doing more, but they've told me to stay out of it. It does seem like they're my best bet."

"I'm not convinced of that." Then he sighed. "But I don't have much faith in the City anymore, either. The fact that Council is pushing forward with regulations about breeders, cats and who knows what else without proper consultation concerns me. I suspect even the police are in league with Bill Bradshaw."

"Probably," she said. "Leaders and cops usually are."

His disappointment in the City was probably what had kept him from pressing harder on going to the authorities about the exotic pet ring. Like Cori, Jon always put animal welfare first. Unlike Cori, it made him uncomfortable to flout the laws. Luckily, the capybara pup was flourishing in his care—so much so, he'd told Evie he was afraid it wouldn't bond properly with its littermates when they were reunited.

Touching his arm, she said, "Why don't we push all of that out of our minds for a few hours? Tomorrow we have the Easter festival rehearsal, and I'm quite sure we'll hash this subject to pieces."

"With City staff around?" he asked.

She shook her head. "The mayor pulled Zeke and most of the staff to support a fundraiser in Wychwood Grove that he didn't want to attend himself. So I had to rely on the goodwill of friends to set up the grounds at Dayton Manor." It had surprised her that Cori, Bridget and the others had readily agreed to come out, considering there was no love lost with the City, but they responded without hesitation. "I half-wonder if the mayor wants this event to fail," she said. "But he's sending enough people on Sunday to make sure it isn't a big enough flop to hit the papers."

"I don't get it," Jon said. "I've always liked Zeke and I don't know why he's going along with all this."

"I'm sure there's something in it for him. An appointment, perhaps. Or a great job with one of the mayor's cronies. He's ambitious."

Jon turned the van into the main parking lot at the foot of the official trail system—miles from where she'd met up with the mafia the other night. His expression brightened as soon as he opened the door.

"I need some fresh air," he said. "There's nothing like a walk in the hills to make you fall in love with Dog Town again."

He unhooked Gilda's leash and she took off like a shot.

For the next hour, she was always ahead of them or above them, chasing rabbits or squirrels or nothing at all. It did Evie's soul good to watch her play. She wished she could do the same. But her cares would be waiting for her at the end of the walk, a weight far heavier than Roberto between her shoulder blades.

Beautiful weather had brought people out in droves. Jon was stopped frequently by dog owners and re-introduced to past patients, now the picture of health. His spirits rose, too, and he was smiling and happy by the time they turned back.

"Hello, Evelyn," someone called.

She turned and saw Clarence Dayton. He was making good time down the trail for someone his age. After introducing Jon, she asked, "Any second thoughts on attending the Easter festival?"

"Second, third, and twentieth thoughts... all with the same outcome," he said, with a rare smile. "I wouldn't get near it if my life depended on it."

"Would it make a difference if I told you the mayor may skip it? He's going to an ashram for the weekend."

"Perfect place for an ass," Clarence said. "Still not biting."

"Understood," she said, smiling. "Well, I won't keep you from enjoying this lovely day."

"Go home to your cat," he said, carrying on. "He's probably lonely."

They walked around a bend and Jon asked, "You told him about Roberto?"

She shook her head. "Word gets around, I guess. Clarence isn't as big a hermit as I thought."

Later, they drove back into the city and Jon took her to a popular restaurant near the museum. While Gilda snoozed in the van, they walked into the Bone Appetit

Bistro. The place was nothing fancy, but it was fun to see Bridget Linsmore, the assistant manager, buzzing around and serving more tables than anyone else. After delivering their Doggone Burgers—a house specialty—Bridget barely had time to chat again. But when they left, she grabbed Evie's arm and whispered, "Don't worry. It'll all come up roses and Easter eggs. You'd be surprised by how fortune favors the good in Dog Town. It just puts us through hell first."

When they got back to the van, Gilda greeted them with a lazy wag and a few licks.

"Shall we finish with a stroll on the boardwalk?" Jon asked. "There's going to be a full moon."

Evie sighed. "It sounds lovely, but I want to get home to Roberto. I managed to push him out of my mind for awhile but he's creeping back in."

"Pets first," he said. "Always."

He held her hand for the rest of the drive, and she enjoyed the quiet warmth without speaking. Usually she chatted compulsively on first dates, but with Jon things were easy. She warned herself again not to get too attached. If she got fired by the City, it would likely be difficult to find a good job in Dog Town. She might have to move on again, and that would be easier if she hadn't formed attachments. At least she'd have Roberto this time. Somehow that made the prospect less gloomy.

The full moon was rising when they pulled up in front of her house. Still low on the horizon, it was enormous and deep orange... the color of a marmalade cat.

Jon got out, opened her door and took her hand to help her out. He linked his fingers through hers while walking her to the porch. At the foot of the stairs, he tugged on her hand to make her turn.

"Thank you for such a lovely time," she said, smiling up at him. "I felt like a carefree child again for a few hours."

"Me too." He smiled, but his eyes seemed to be searching her face. Perhaps he was also debating in his mind whether to go any further with this right now. She didn't want to sway him either way.

Jon's hesitation passed. Leaning forward, he pulled her up on her tiptoes and she had a feeling of weightlessness and giddy excitement. The second his lips touched hers, she knew she'd been fooling herself. The tingles she'd felt days ago turned into starbursts, followed by a warm golden glow that filled her from head to foot. Jon wasn't like Surf and Turf, or any of the other men she'd left behind. He was special, and things were going to get complicated. When the kiss ended, she slipped her arm around his neck for a hug. Over his shoulder, her eyes filled as they scanned up to find the full moon. There was no such thing as a curse, of course, but sometimes it felt like it. Would she ever be able to let go and enjoy a relationship?

Her gaze reached the moon and dropped suddenly. Something wasn't quite right with the house. It looked like the door was slightly ajar.

Pushing Jon away, she rushed up the stairs. "I... I think there's been a break-in."

He took the stairs two at a time and brushed past her. The door had been forced. It probably hadn't taken much, given the state of the house.

"Stay here," he said, pushing the door open with his elbow. "Don't touch anything."

She followed him inside anyway, and as he circled the kitchen and living room, she bolted up the stairs. "Roberto? You okay?"

"Evie, wait!" He thumped up the stairs after her. "Someone could still be in the house."

She was standing in the open doorway of her bedroom. "Oh, Jon. Roberto is gone."

He moved her aside gently and went into the room. Not only was the cat gone, but his litter box and bowls as well. Kibble crunched underfoot as they moved.

This time the cat hadn't escaped. He'd been taken.

"Don't panic," Jon said. "If they took his stuff, they don't mean him any harm."

"But why?" she said, tears sliding down her cheeks. "Why would someone steal my cat?"

He slipped an arm around her shoulders and guided her downstairs. "I don't know. Is it possible the original owner saw that photo of him on the roof and reclaimed him?"

"Why wouldn't they just ask?" she said. "I'd have given him back, even if it broke my heart."

"What about the mayor? You said he wanted you to surrender Roberto. Maybe he sent over the CCD."

"Maybe," she said, almost hopefully. If so, Kinney could find out and find him. Looking around the house, she shuddered. "If the City did this, I'll have to quit."

"Let's not get ahead of ourselves," he said. "It's just one theory."

She left his side and went to the front door, examining it for clues. There was nothing amiss with the doorknob on either side. But when she leaned in to look at the frame, a chill ran down her spine. There were deep grooves in the wood from two sets of claws. Dropping to her knees, she saw a few drops of fresh blood on the floor and another outside on the porch.

Roberto hadn't left without a fight.

Kneeling beside her, Jon gave a low growl. "Who would do such a thing... hurt an innocent cat?"

"Someone raising and burying exotic pets," she said, rubbing tears away with her sleeve. "Maybe they decided he was too much of a liability."

He got to his feet and pulled out his phone. "I'm calling the police."

She grabbed his hand. "No. I'll call Kinney and Cori instead. They've got the connections to figure this out."

Pulling his hand away, he said, "Evie, this has gone far enough. Someone broke into your home. You're not safe."

"They got what they wanted, which was to steal the cat and possibly scare me." She stepped out on the porch to pull in a few breaths of cool night air. It felt like she was going to suffocate inside. "But if they think I'm giving up on Roberto, they're wrong."

He blew out a frustrated sigh. "I'm not on board with this, Evie. I asked you to get help sooner—before the cat was collateral damage."

"I know. I'm sorry I dragged you into it. But I'm so far down the road now that I can't turn back. I will fix this, Jon, I promise."

"You can't promise that."

He started down the stairs and she reached for his arm. "I do promise. I will get Roberto back and rescue the rest of the animals."

At the bottom of the stairs, he stared up at her with wide blue eyes. "How exactly do you plan to pull that off?"

"You'll just need to trust me. I know I can make it right. I just know it." She wasn't lying. Somewhere, deep in her heart, she found assurance that she could fix this problem. In fact, it felt like she already knew the answer, if only she could put the pieces together properly.

"That's not much to go on. In fact, it sounds crazy."

"Just give me two days. If it's not fixed by Easter, I promise to call in every possible authority and the media to boot. You said yourself that they wouldn't take Roberto's stuff if they meant to hurt him."

Jon rubbed both hands over his face and through his hair until it stood on end. "Get in the van," he said. "We're going to check on the other animals. Then you're staying with me until Easter."

Evie shook her head. "I want to be here in case Roberto comes home. If he can escape my place, maybe he can escape his captor's."

Coming back up the stairs, he grabbed her hand and it wasn't quite so gentle this time. "Edit that. We'll check on the animals, collect my stuff and then I'll sleep on your couch till Easter. I'm so angry right now I could spit, Evie, but I'm not leaving you here alone."

That only made her cry even harder as she followed him down the stairs.

CHAPTER TWENTY-THREE

Many hands made light work of the festival prep on Saturday afternoon. Remi and her friends Arden Lee and Flynn Strathmore took over decorations, dressing up and festooning the stone statuary with items they'd picked up in thrift stores. Medusa became far less intimidating in a huge purple fright wig and a yellow strapless frock, and the satyr was positively jaunty in moth-eaten gray tails and a red cravat. Meanwhile, Kinney and Cori worked with some of the men to stretch chicken wire over the gardens. Since they didn't know which ones might contain old bones, they covered them all. Remi's beau, Tiller Iverson, was a professional landscaper and he knew how to do the job without making it ugly and obvious. Bridget and Duff set up a long table near the manor to support an assembly line for egg-stuffing. Evie worked alongside them, as well as Nika, Maisie, and Sasha, to unscrew the hard plastic eggs and fill them with scraps of meat. Then they stored the eggs in coolers. It wouldn't be safe to hide them all over the grounds till morning, along with all the candy and toys for the young humans.

There should have been laughter—and here and there, a few chuckles rang out—but mostly the mood was somber. Everyone offered hushed consolation to Evie about Roberto, and Mim Gardiner, the nurse she'd visited with the cat, stuck by her side. The previous Christmas, Mim's dog had been abducted, but happily George was here today, frolicking with all the other dogs. In fact, dogs outnumbered the humans. Ari had brought along Thurston Howl.

"I thought he might cheer you up," she said, as Evie knelt in the damp grass to pat the wriggly, curly dog. "Although I'm not your biggest fan since you offered me up like a liver treat to the dog breeders. Leann insists I represent them all to the mayor, and I have a one-on-one with him on Tuesday."

"Really? That's wonderful." Perhaps it shouldn't surprise her that Zeke and the mayor had agreed to that without consulting her, but it still did. "You'll do well, Ari. The mayor is all about keeping it chill right now, and you have a lovely manner."

"Not to mention a lovely face," Bridget said, snipping prosciutto into tiny squares with kitchen shears. "I'm sure that won't be lost on the mayor, despite his spiritual pursuits. I had to get a makeover to get his attention for the pageant. Now I can let myself go till November."

Bridget was a natural beauty, with her hair in a messy knot and nothing but lip balm on her face. Meanwhile, Ari's golden hair flowed in loose waves, and her makeup was totally on point. Even her casual clothing looked runway-ready. The mayor would love her, and there was a chance—albeit a slim one—that her words would also make an impression.

By then, hopefully the Easter festival would be a grand success and front-page news. Children and dogs would frolic all over the grounds, and make the pall that hung over the estate dissipate. Even today, it didn't seem so macabre, now that she'd met Clarence and heard its history. As eccentric as the family had been, they were animal lovers and rescuers on a large scale.

Their work was almost done when a red BMW convertible pulled into the parking lot. Zeke Mackey was at the wheel, and beside him, hair blowing into knots, was Chloe, their receptionist. For once she was not wearing earbuds.

He got out of the car and joked around with the men before joining Evie. "That's a lot of chicken wire," he said, looking at the gardens.

Evie pointed to the crocuses pushing through. "Just protecting the bulbs from the dogs. Some of these flowers date back to the Daytons' time, you know."

"Another myth," he said. "This place is full of them. But I must admit you've done a fine job. Looks like you don't even need Chloe and me. We left the fundraiser early to lend a hand."

"Aw, how sweet," she said. Chloe was standing near the car in a pretty white dress. Lending a hand probably wasn't in her plan. "I think we're good."

"Suit yourself." Leaning down, he whispered, "Looks like you've got the Mafia eating out of your hand."

She shook her head, laughing. "Only if I want to lose a hand, which I don't."

"Well, watch a pro work," he said. Turning, he called out, "Thanks for all the help, people. This is a perfect example of the community spirit Dorset Hills is known for. We'll remember it as we move forward with new initiatives, like the service dog center of excellence. I'd say we have all the expertise we need for it right here today."

Before his car was even out of the parking lot, Cori

collapsed on the grass giving fake dry heaves. "If that's our next mayoral candidate, I'll have no choice but to run," she said.

"Oh, Zeke's not so bad," Tiller Iverson said. "Not much of a hockey player, but a good sport."

Cori glared at him and said, "Remi deserves better."

He just laughed. "I couldn't agree more. I hope she never realizes."

Evie got Cori to help her load some coolers into the car. "I heard you hang with Clarence Dayton," she said.

"Who told you that?" Cori's voice was sharp.

"Clarence himself. I visited to see if he'd come out for Easter and bless this event. And to get a look at his place, of course."

"I'm only hearing about this now?"

Evie shrugged. "We had a lot on the agenda the other day. Anyway, it was just another dead end. I didn't learn anything there."

Cori trudged back to the manor, scowling. "I hope you learned how Clarence got ripped off by the City. There's a long history of treating rescuers like crap, but he got the worst of it, losing this place."

"I know. I didn't know the story before I went. I ended up feeling sorry for him. He's all alone."

"He's not alone. He has Ramona, and occasional litters of kittens that I find homes for. And he has Bridget and me. We stop by often."

"Kindred spirits," Evie said. "I'm glad you're looking out for him."

An hour later, Jon joined them after his clinic ended, and though he was still a bit dour, he dropped a kiss on her cheek, and went to join the guys. Evie watched him sadly, wondering if they'd get over this obstacle. He was a good man, and she'd gotten unexpectedly attached to him in a short time. She blamed part of that on Gilda. The big dog seemed to realize she was grieving, and instead of rough-housing with the other dogs, kept shoving her head under Evie's hand for a pat.

"Now, that's a good dog," Bridget said, eying Gilda. "She thinks she's human, just like Beau."

"That's not exclusive to dogs," Evie said. "Roberto thought he was people, too."

"Thinks," Mim said. "Present tense. He's still out there scheming, I'm sure of it."

Flynn Strathmore finished twisting streamers around a mid-sized ogre and asked, "What does your intuition tell you, Evie? Sometimes we sense things."

"Flynn's got magical powers," Remi said, smiling. "She practically imagined her dog Mo into being."

"Just luck," Flynn said. But her serious gaze said other-wise, and it prompted Evie to close her eyes for a second to see if she could pick up any sense of Roberto. An odd sensation prickled between her shoulder blades, as if he'd landed there again. If it was a message, it made her wince and smile at the same time.

"Cut the woo-woo crap," Cori said, joining them. "Let's focus on what we *can* do, instead of hoping for miracles."

"Well, what *can* we do?" Evie asked. "I looked all over the neighborhood for him this morning. I even tried putting up signs but someone kept ripping them down. Thirty posters are gone already. The neighborhood cleanup committee apparently hates cats."

"Idiots," Cori said, in disgust. "Thank goodness we have a plan."

"We do?"

"We do," Remi said, smiling. "Hannah Pemberton is coming home today for the street party."

"What street party?"

"The one on your street," Remi said. "Hosted by you."

A grin passed from one face to another until Evie herself smiled uncertainly. "I don't get it."

"It doesn't seem like the time to host a street party," Jon said, joining them. "But I'm guessing there's a notorious mafia plan behind this."

"Notorious," Cori said. "I like that. We're the gangsters of rescue."

"Cori," Duff said. "Jon may not share our notorious sense of humor."

"He does," Evie said. "He's just worried that things are out of hand."

"They're not out of hand," Cori said, glaring at Jon.

"They're out of hand," Remi said.

Cori turned her glare on Remi. "This is why you're not a full-fledged mafia member."

"Even though the street party idea was mostly my idea? And the sponsor of it was *entirely* my idea?"

"Well, you gained some points, there," Cori admitted. "But your tolerance for risk is shockingly low."

"Despite my shockingly risky proposal," Remi said, putting her hands on her hips.

Cori made a face. "It was out of character. So bonus points for that."

Leo emerged from a mass of roughhousing dogs to sit at Remi's feet. "It's okay, Leo," she said. "Cori's backing down."

"Curious," Kinney said, smirking. "I'm not sure I've seen that happen before."

"It's very rare," Bridget said. "But it does happen."

Evie cleared her throat. "Can someone share this shockingly risky plan that involves my hosting a street party? A party that I can't afford and don't have the wherewithal to organize?"

"All you need to do is step out of your house at eight sharp and plaster on a big fake smile," Cori said. "Can you do that?"

"Of course," Evie said. "I work in politics. My speciality is big fake smiles."

"Bring your best game," Cori said. "Because you'll be working the crowd like you mean to run for office yourself."

"Never," Evie said. "Cori Hogan for mayor."

The grin that had stayed on most faces now transformed into a laugh as the crowd dispersed. Flynn beckoned Evie and pulled her sketchbook out of the back of her car. Tearing out a page, she offered her a sketch of Roberto. He stared out at her with one ragged ear, his tail wrapped neatly around his paws. He looked composed, smug even, and there was a big fish locked in his jaws.

"Oh wow," Evie said, shivering despite the warm breeze. "It looks just like him, right down to the ragged ear. But what's with the fish?"

Flynn shrugged. "I don't know. My pencil has a mind of its own."

"Well thank you," Evie said, rolling up the sketch carefully. "Nice to see him with another catch."

Before getting into her car, she stared back at the gaily decorated statues, now under plastic tarps, and watched the dogs kibitz as their owners called them to leave. Despite what had happened, it felt like one of the best days of her life.

If only it hadn't followed one of the worst.

CHAPTER TWENTY-FOUR

E vie was out working the crowd long before the party's official kickoff at eight that evening. Hannah Pemberton was her co-host, and that was enough to bring out everyone onto the street. The same crowd from earlier was out in full force to set up folding tables that caterers filled with food. There was even an open bar that wasn't legal, but the neighborhood committee didn't seem to have an issue with that.

As she made her rounds with Hannah, Evie said, "I'm not sure exactly what's going on, but I know it's to help me, so... thank you."

"You're very welcome," Hannah said. She was probably the wealthiest person in town at that moment, but with her long dark ponytail, jeans and sneakers, she looked no different from her hometown friend, Remi. "I don't know the full plan either, and it's probably better that way. Our mission, if you choose to accept it, is to keep the crowd here and focussed on free food and drink. There's a band on the way, as well."

"And what's everyone else doing?" Evie turned in time

to see Jon getting towed off by Bridget's boyfriend, Sullivan Shaw. Carver Black, Mim's beau, was waiting for them near the bushes. Everyone was in black except Jon, and he slipped his arms into a dark jacket Bridget offered.

Cori flitted by, also entirely in black, except for the orange middle fingers of her gloves. They were obvious when she beckoned to Remi, who silently kissed Leo's head before handing him over to Hannah.

"Be careful," Hannah said, as Leo settled happily into the crook of her arm. Remi waved and disappeared into the shadows with Cori. One by one, the others left their stations and joined them. It was almost as if it were choreographed, which it probably was.

By this point, the crowd was so dense that you had to be paying close attention to see them leave. Jon reappeared for a moment and pressed Gilda's leash into her hand. "Be good," he said, leaning in to kiss Evie's cheek.

"Me, or the dog?" she asked.

"Both." His grin was heartening. She hadn't seen it for what seemed like forever, but was only twenty-four hours. "Rock your street party."

Soon the only familiar face was Hannah's, besides the few neighbors she'd met briefly in passing. But the crowds thickened quickly, as news of the party spread. People came on foot, in cars, and even minivans packed full. There were kids and seniors and everyone in between. And there were dogs... so many dogs that Evie worried fights would break out. None did. Instead, some played on lawns, others begged for pats, and the rest mooched by the food stations.

Every time a new wave of people came in, Hannah got on the phone and ordered more food and booze.

"Aren't you worried about the police?" Evie asked.

Hannah shook her head. "Ari's dating a cop. He told

everyone to turn a blind eye unless things got out of hand. But they won't get out of hand, because some of his friends are here in plain clothes."

"This took some planning," Evie said.

"I believe they're calling it Operation Ocelot," Hannah said. "Maybe that means more to you than it does to me."

Evie nodded. "It's bigger than Roberto."

"Well, don't tell me. I'm one of those people who's happy to play the role they've been given. The less I know, the less I can mess up."

"Good point," Evie said, pulling in a deep breath. "Shall we continue?"

With leashes in one hand, they got back to mingling. Everywhere they turned, people reached out to meet Hannah, and she quickly introduced them to Evie. Meanwhile Evie smiled so hard it felt as if her face would shatter.

Finally, a large hand stretched out and this time, it was to shake hers. "Oh," she said, looking up. "Zeke. What are you doing here?"

"Neighborhood party, right?" he said.

"Right. For my neighborhood."

"Well, someone came to the door to invite me. The pretty blonde breeder you've assigned to work her wiles on the mayor."

"Oh, Zeke," she said. "As if Ari—or anyone—could distract the mayor from his spiritual path."

"True," he said. "But she's welcome to try." He turned and scanned the crowd. "Where's Hannah Pemberton?"

"Ah, that's why you're here."

He gave her a knowing smile. "I'm here for the open bar. The illegal one the off-duty cops don't seem to mind."

"I let my friends set things up for me, so I could just hang out with the locals."

Looking down, he gestured to Gilda. "What's this? Your security detail?"

Evie hadn't even noticed that the dog had moved in front of her. And when Zeke shifted position, Gilda did, too. It was subtle, but noticeable. The dog was clearly picking up on her anxiety about losing her job.

"She's a sweetheart," Evie said. "Crowds just make her nervous. Now, go work your wiles on Hannah."

"Yes, boss," he said, smirking.

Soon he had Hannah cornered between a minivan and a convertible, and was talking her ear off. Hannah's smile was as bright as ever, but her fingers flew over Leo's head again and again. After a few minutes, the beagle adjusted position to nestle under her chin. Oblivious, Zeke talked on. Whether he was pitching for the city or himself, Evie didn't know, and didn't care. She had other fish to fry, as Cori had suggested they divide and conquer.

An hour later, her fingers ached from all the handshakes and it was a relief when the band set up. Soon, people were clapping and dancing, and two big guys, who were probably police officers, helped shut down the bar.

Hannah found her way back and handed Leo over to Evie. "You look like you could use a hit of this beagle."

"I could," she said, hoping Leo wasn't worn out. On the contrary, he lounged in her arms and let his ears flop fetchingly. Gilda looked up reproachfully, and Evie reassured her. "Don't worry, girl, you're my first canine love."

"But not your last, I bet," Hannah said. "I thought the whole concept of Dog Town was ridiculous on my first trip home. Now I'm on Ari's waiting list for a pup."

"That would be my choice, too," Evie said. "If I could handle a pup, which I clearly can't."

"Don't be so hard on yourself. Crazy things happen in

this town. All we can do is respond as best we can." Her smile was calm and beautiful, like Mona Lisa's, only sweeter.

"So, you're moving back for real?"

Hannah gazed around, her expression weary. "Probably. This place is too much sometimes, but it would be a good place to raise a family."

"I didn't realize you were seeing someone," Evie said.

"I'm not." She laughed a little. "I'll worry about the details later."

"Well, there's Zeke," Evie said, hoping her voice didn't betray her true feelings.

Hannah rolled her eyes. "That guy has gold-digger written all over him. And trust me, I've seen it before. I'm not worried about finding a guy. I want a community."

"Well, we have that already, don't we?" Evie said.

Several people loomed out of the darkness, and one of them turned out to be Jon. He came over to Evie and slipped an arm around her shoulders. She didn't need to ask if there was any good news. His expression was as weary as Hannah's.

Cori stood watching from the bushes, and didn't move until Zeke finally drifted off in a group of men in golf shirts and khakis. Then she came over to Evie and shook her head. "No sign of Roberto, or the exotics," she said. "We split up in pairs and covered every house for a six-block radius. That's about all the territory we figured a cat could cover at a dead run from your place."

Tears welled up in Evie's eyes, partly from sorrow over Roberto, and partly from gratitude that these people—acquaintances of just weeks—would put themselves at risk for her.

"Thank you for—"

"Stop. We didn't do it for you," Cori said, looking away. "We did it for the animals. And we didn't succeed, yet. But we will." When she turned back there was a cheeky smile on her face. "I always get my man. I'm notorious."

"And nefarious," Duff said, joining them.

"And infamous," Remi said.

"Wicked," Kinney added.

Cori glared at her. "Hey."

"What? Wicked's good, right?"

Once again, Evie had that odd sensation of being lifted, even while her heart was dashed.

"Let's get you inside and to bed," Jon said. "Tonight it was your street, and tomorrow you host the entire city."

She zipped her jacket up tight and said, "Would you mind if we took a walk first? I feel too wound up to sleep and a stroll would help me switch channels."

Jon took her hand and they set off down the road with Gilda trotting happily at her side.

"When did my dog transfer allegiance to you?" he asked, surrendering the leash before it tripped her.

"She's more in tune than a trained therapy dog, you know. I think she'd give Leo a run for his money, if only she could be carried around like a handbag."

"You're right," he said. "I'd get her certified for therapy work if I had the time. She'd love to visit seniors' homes and schools."

"That's my next life, I hope," she said, squeezing his hand. "I see the magic these dogs work for people and I want to make more of that happen. Somehow. Maybe it's a training school, where we certify dogs for people in need. People with disabilities, people with trauma, kids with peanut allergies, you name it. And all free."

Jon pulled her arm through his. "It sounds like a big undertaking, but I have complete faith you could pull it off."

She looked up at the stars and sighed. "Call me crazy, but it feels like that might be my life's work."

"I'd never call you crazy," he said.

"You already called me crazy."

"Correction: I'd never call you crazy and mean it."

Looking around, she said, "Where are we? I don't recall being here but it looks vaguely familiar."

"Not sure, but I covered it earlier, with the gang. I only saw backyards."

"How come I couldn't be in the yard crew?" she asked. "It would have been more fun than glad-handing the neighborhood."

"Evie, it was the best use of your talents." He kissed the side of her head. "Plus, you're accident prone and we were scaling fences. Thank goodness most dogs were at the party. We skipped a couple with bulldogs on sentry."

"I probably would have ended up impaled and on the front pages."

"Well, you didn't miss much," he said, but his eyes sparkled like a kid's. "Some of these places back onto the ravine and the brush is as thick as a forest. I think I heard coyotes."

"Coyotes? In Dorset Hills?"

"Why not? There are wolves in sheep's clothing."

He was still chuckling at his own joke when Gilda put on the brakes. "What's up, girl?" Evie said. "Do you hear a coyote?"

The dog was clearly agitated. She turned to face the closest house, a blocky brick two-story, with the usual twisted twig dog on the lawn. After listening for a moment, she did a deep play bow.

"Come on, Gilda," Jon said. "It's too late for games."

The dog spun a full turn and did a second play pose.

That was when they heard the keening of a wild dog rising toward the overcast sky.

"Yikes," Evie said, as goosebumps prickled all over. "Let's get out of here."

They turned to go, but Gilda kept trying to pull back. She actually plunked down in the middle of an intersection at one point.

"It's like The Call of the Wild," Jon said, when they finally reached Evie's driveway.

Something on the lawn caught her eye. Garbage from the party, she figured. The grass had grown and greened up quickly in the past two weeks. Now something was almost hidden in it.

"Look, look! It's orange." She pointed as the words spilled out fast and high. "Is it Roberto?"

Dropping Gilda's leash she ran across the lawn. Just before she got there, she tripped over something and fell flat on her face. She crawled the last few feet.

The cat was splayed out on its side, unmoving. Her breath caught in her throat as she reached out.

"Wait," Jon said, leaning over. "This doesn't look good. I want you to sit up and turn away, Evie."

She did as she was told, wrapping her arms around her knees and shaking uncontrollably. "Is it him? Is he alive?"

"No," Jon said.

"It's not him? Or it's not alive?"

"Both. This cat hasn't been alive in some time. Decades, perhaps."

She pushed herself up and turned. Jon was holding a stiff cat in both hands. It looked like it was posed, ready to pounce.

"What the—?" she said.

"Taxidermy."

"What is a stuffed dead cat doing on my lawn?" She rubbed trembling hands over her face, and then reached for Gilda. The dog moved closer and pressed her head against Evie's shoulder.

"Another threat, I'm afraid," Jon said. "This just gets more disturbing by the day. Are you still convinced you can get to the bottom of it tomorrow?"

"Yes," she said, knowing the quaver in her voice betrayed her. Straightening her shoulders, she turned. "Can you get a picture of this to send to Kinney and Cori, and then... put it somewhere safe? It's time for extreme measures," she said.

If only she knew exactly what those measures would be.

CHAPTER TWENTY-FIVE

"Are you kidding me? Are you freaking kidding me, Evie?"

"Oh hey, Nick." She was pouring herself a second cup of coffee when her brother called on Easter morning. "What's up?"

"What's up? What's *up*?"

"You're repeating yourself. Are you okay?"

"Am I *okay*? There's a weird-looking animal in a cage in my dining room and my house stinks to high heaven. Ask me again if I'm okay."

"Oh. You're home." She beckoned urgently to Jon, who was eating cereal at the kitchen table. "Why didn't you tell me you'd changed your mind?"

"I wanted to surprise you. But instead, you surprised the heck out of me. There's nothing like a big yellow snake in your bathroom to say 'welcome home.'"

"You brought the python back?" she asked Jon.

He nodded. "I wanted it to be closer while I was staying here. The capy's with a colleague."

"Do these animals belong to Jon Benson?" Nick

demanded. "I hear his voice. Put the phone on speaker. Right now."

She pressed the button and the din of crazed barking drowned out whatever Nick said next.

"Is that Clive barking?" she asked.

"Yeah. He's trying to kill that big-eyed stinky thing. In case you're wondering."

"Don't let it out of the cage," Jon said. "I'm not sure what would happen."

"Don't let it... Are you kidding me, Jon? Like I would ever let that weird raccoon loose in my home. Clive would... Well, it wouldn't end well, would it?"

"Not for one of them, anyway. But my clinic's always open."

There was a pause with only barking, and then Nick said, "You're funny. A funny man who is going to sustain personal injury if he doesn't get over here and collect his freaking menagerie."

"Beg your pardon, but the menagerie is your sister's. I'm just the keeper."

There was another pause as Nick shouted at Clive. There was an edge of hysteria in his voice that made Evie want to laugh hysterically, too. She bit her lip to keep it together. This was not the time for hysteria.

"Nick. Just step into your backyard with Clive for a few minutes. We're on our way."

"Don't hang up," he said. There was more shouting at the dog, the sound of a screen door slamming and finally, quiet. "I don't want to be alone with that snake. Not even outside."

"It's a harmless python," Jon said. "At least right now. At full growth it could definitely—"

"Jon." Evie sliced her index finger across her throat as she grabbed her purse. "He's got a thing about snakes."

"Everyone's got a thing about big-ass pythons," Nick grumbled. "It's primal."

"They're fascinating," Jon said, holding the phone as he jumped down Evie's front stairs. "If you can just—"

"Well, I can't. Whatever you're going to propose, I can't. So get it out of here before I call the cops. And the fire department. And the CCD. And every guy on my hockey team. Plus the mayor, too."

"Oh Nick, calm down," Evie said, swinging into the passenger seat when the van was already in reverse. "We're almost there. That snake didn't come near me when it was loose in the living room. It was calm as a kitten. Well, a calm kitten. Not like Roberto."

"Whose living room?" Her brother's tone was ominously quiet now.

"My point is, the snake was calm when it was free."

"It was loose in my house, wasn't it? *Wasn't it?* Now it knows its way around."

"It's not going anywhere. It's safely locked in an aquarium."

"Terrarium," Jon corrected. "It just ate, too. It has no interest in hockey players."

"*Jon.*" Evie glared at him. "Stop teasing. Nick has every right to be upset."

"Damn right I do," her brother said. "All I wanted was for you to check the house, Evie. If you want to collect weird animals, that's your right, but do it at your own house."

"Keep your voice down," she said. "The neighbors have ears."

"Seems like most of them are sleeping off the massive

street party you threw last night," he said. "Thanks for the invitation, by the way. Oh, wait… I wasn't invited."

The van turned into his driveway and she jumped out. "It was a spur-of-the-moment thing. Hannah Pemberton was really the host."

"Hannah Pemberton?" His tone changed. "*Hot* Hannah Pemberton?"

"Leave Hannah alone," she said, walking through the alley beside his house. "She's my friend now, and that makes her off limits."

"Since when?"

"Since forever. Just like you chased off your friends who liked me."

"That's different. I was worried about them because you're cursed."

She unlatched the fence and went into his yard. Nick was standing on top of the picnic table, with Clive beside him on a short leash. His face lit up as he saw her and he lowered the phone.

"You're right, I am cursed," she said, dropping her phone into her purse. "Now come inside so I can explain everything."

"Not till Jon puts his zoo in his van."

"He can't. It's too hot. But he's moving them into your garage."

"My garage? Oh my goodness, Evie!"

She ushered him into the kitchen. "I didn't know your voice even went that high."

They sat down at the kitchen table and she filled him in on all that had happened since he left town. For once, her smart-mouthed brother was actually speechless. At the end, he said simply, "Why didn't you call me home?"

"I wanted to handle it," she said. "I didn't want to embarrass you by getting fired again."

"Evie." His face was serious for once. "I may tease you, but you never embarrass me. You're my little sister."

She rolled her eyes even as they teared up. "Don't start."

"I feel bad," he said. "You came to this town for a fresh start because of me, and now someone is threatening you. Leaving a dead cat on your lawn is serious business."

"Just a taxidermy. That's not so serious."

She smiled to lighten the mood, but her brother's eyes were full of storm clouds.

"It is serious because it's demented," he said. "Who would do that?"

"The kind of person who raises exotic pets, I guess."

"Right. So, demented. And that person was in your home and stole your cat. What's next?"

"Well, they obviously want me to back off."

"But you're not backing off, are you? Instead, you're escalating things. A street party and a posse of backyard investigators isn't going to stop the madness." He leaned back in his seat and crossed his arms. "What's the next move?"

"I don't know. Cori and the mafia are cooking something up."

"I don't like this. Two many cooks in the kitchen."

Jon came in from the garage. "Who's cooking?"

"I am," Nick said. "We're having honey bear stew."

"Don't even joke about that. I'm sensitive about my animals." He sat down at the table with them and his smile faded. "I just got an email from the lab about those bones, Evie. There was a mixture of very old bones from the Daytons' days, and some from the last couple of years. Mostly young animals. Breeding failures, I assume."

"What kind of animals?" She stopped. "Never mind. I don't want to picture them."

Nick tapped his fingers on the table. "Evie, did you bring your laptop? Let me check the footage from the cat cam."

She pulled it out of her bag. "It's corrupted. We've tried half a dozen times and a friend of Kinney's tried, too."

He cracked his knuckles theatrically. "Who's your hacker, now?"

As a teenager, Nick had routinely hacked into buddies' computers and printed X-rated images just to shock their mothers. She knew there was more to his antics, but nowadays he played it straight and clean because his reputation depended on it.

She checked her messages while she waited, and found a flurry of texts on a group chat from the rescue mafia. Operation Ocelot was about all she understood. There was a code they hadn't shared. Well, she'd find out soon at the festival, she guessed.

"And... I got it," Nick said, pumping his fist.

He angled the laptop so she could see and Jon moved behind them. Nick cued up the fractured images he'd recovered. Watching was dizzying, as the cat appeared to be jumping around, on top of crates containing various creatures. At one point, he circled what appeared to be the honey bear. He jumped up and then down, and they saw his orange paws working at the big metal clasp.

"Well, I'll be damned," Jon said. "He freed the kinkajou himself. I underestimated that cat."

"Me too," Evie said. "He picked something he could carry. He's part of the rescue mafia."

There was a skirmish as Roberto tried to grab the honey

bear, and a terrified squeal that made both men look away. Evie leaned in closer to catch every move.

And that was when she saw it. Behind the cage was an old desk, and above that hung something she recognized.

"What?" Jon said, squeezing her shoulder. "You're pale. Did you see something?"

Shaking her head, she summoned her very best fake smile. It had never been faker than at this moment. "It's just all too much. Seeing what Roberto was willing to do to save these animals..."

"He's a cat," Nick said. "I think he just found a nice squeaky toy to play with."

"You don't know this cat," she said. "I've got to find him and bring him home."

"Let's get this Easter festival out of the way so we can keep trying," Jon said.

Her smile stretched until it felt like an instant face lift. "Grab your Easter bonnet, brother, and let's get going."

"Can you stop smiling like that?" Nick asked. "You'll scare the honey bear."

"Not the snake, though," Jon said. "They find big smiles very s-s-s-soothing. You need to smile more, Nick."

They split up to get ready, and Nick and Jon were still jokingly shoving each other as they climbed into the van. Evie was glad that their bickering kept them from noticing she was deep in thought.

Finally, she knew exactly where to go. She just needed to figure out what to do when she got there.

CHAPTER TWENTY-SIX

Dorset Hills loved nothing more than a parade, but the new Easter festival was turning out to be a contender. People of all ages had come out with their dogs, and children raced around, even hugging statues that might have terrified them were it not for the fun costumes and streamers. The large property had been divided into sections for the Easter egg hunt, with makeshift fencing to keep the dogs away from the kids' candy and the kids away from the dogs' prosciutto. The kids' hunt was first on the agenda, as there would be no peace otherwise. Then there would be games, photos with the Easter bunny, refreshments, and finally, the main event: the dogs' Easter hunt.

All members of the extended mafia were on hand to oversee the action, moving with military precision to keep children and dogs out of mischief. Duff, Remi and Flynn handled the adults, while Mim, Sasha, Arden and Hannah wrangled the kids. Cori, Bridget, Nika and Maisie were tasked with keeping more than a hundred dogs civil. Luckily they had plenty of help from dog breeders, including Leann, Ruth and Ari. Meanwhile, Kinney worked with the men to orchestrate events and keep people in designated areas. City staff were relegated to the sidelines and soon drifted off to enjoy the event like regular folk.

Evie navigated the crowd with Zeke, who was acting as the host for the City in the mayor's absence. They posed for photos with kids and dogs, and did interviews with reporters for the newspaper and local TV station.

When they had a quiet moment, Zeke said, "I've got to hand it to you, Evie: you really pulled a rabbit out of your hat with this event."

He gestured to a six-foot-tall Easter bunny in a gray plush costume. At the last moment, she'd made a switch from the white costume. She'd never fancied albino bunnies and their pink eyes.

"I had a lot of help," she said, nodding to her friends. "The community spirit in Dog Town astounds me. I hope you realize what you have here."

"Of course. That's why I'll never leave." He gave her a sidelong glance. "How about you?"

"Never say never. But I don't think I could go back to a big city now."

"When all this is over, let's sit down with the mayor," he said. "We threw you into the deep end with the breeders, and we can probably find a role that's more suited to you. Event planning is definitely your forte."

"Thanks, Zeke," she said, rolling out her fake smile once more. "I appreciate that vote of confidence. But you know my passion lies with service dogs."

He gave a lazy wave of his hand. "We'll talk. But not today."

"Agreed," Evie said. "No point talking about work when there are future investors to court. I have it on good authority that Hannah Pemberton is committed to moving here. She'll need help spending her billions here."

Zeke loped away without another word and her rictus smile relaxed.

Hannah caught her eye and nodded. She'd agreed to keep Zeke fully occupied for as long as she could. Remi was playing backup, and would implement whatever measures necessary to keep him from noticing Evie had left the party. As a testament to the strength of their new friendship, both women had agreed to say nothing to the others, most especially Cori. They'd also promised to do their very best to keep things on track. If all went as Evie hoped, the festival would be a huge success and cover the quiet disbandment of an exotic breeding operation. As long as she could move quickly, all could be in hand in two hours.

Walking up to the bunny, she whispered, "May I please speak to you in the bushes?"

When the bunny emerged, no one seemed to notice it was six inches shorter. And after posing for a few photos with townspeople, Evie gradually wove through the crowd. There was a scary moment where she tripped over a foot-high cherub—one she hadn't noticed before—but after a small tumble, she made it to the parking lot unscathed. Retrieving the key she'd stashed over the front wheel, she climbed into Jon's van. The rabbit head was terribly awkward, especially the ears, but she didn't dare remove it until she was clear of the event. Somehow she managed to drive out of the lot without running over people or dogs.

"That would make the front pages," she muttered into the stifling costume. "Easter bunny flattens Dog Town."

Pulling off the head, she pressed a huge paw down on the gas, hip-hopping the van past the bronze St. Bernard and the Dalmatian and into Riverdale. The drive was anything but smooth, but she didn't have a moment to spare.

With difficulty, she backed into the driveway of the house Gilda had stopped at the night before. Pulling the rabbit head back on, she jumped out, and grabbed a hockey bag from the back of the van. Moving with uncharacteristic grace, she slipped around the side of the house. There was a high fence, but a small fruit tree beside it offered a launch pad. It might have gone smoothly, had it not been for the bunny paws. She made it over the fence, but her landing was anything but elegant. The pain that shot through her foot suggested a sprain at minimum, but she didn't let it slow her down.

The entire back of the house was a sunroom with wide-paned windows. She stared up, wondering how best to get inside.

A movement caught her eye, and she adjusted the bunny head to get a better look. Was it...? Could it be...?

Roberto was standing inside on top of what appeared to be an elegant table. When he saw her, he butted his head against the glass so hard she could practically feel it, and his mouth opened in silent meows.

"I'm coming, buddy," she said, knowing her voice would be unintelligible though the costume. "I don't know how, but I'll break you out of there."

She climbed the porch and tried the door, knowing it was fruitless. No one who had an exotic breeding operation would leave the door unlocked. Hanging over the railing, she peered inside. It looked like a perfectly normal living room, with a perfectly normal cat running around like a crazed thing.

Back and forth Roberto ran, as if trying to guide her. Finally, as he disappeared from view once more, she followed him around the side of the house. Dense twigs caught on the costume as she pushed through bushes.

Her phone buzzed in her pocket, and she groaned. Pulling off one furry glove, she groped until she found the way into the costume and grabbed her phone.

"Zeke's starting to break up the party and send people home," Remi texted. "Should I let the dogs out to create a commotion?"

"No. Help is on the way. Go give a speech thanking the mayor and Zeke. Offer him a community award—the stone cherub by the parking lot. Then look out for an incoming special guest who'll give another speech."

She punched in another text and took a shaky breath. It was all she could do, but she might only have half an hour at best before the homeowner returned.

At the side of the house was another tall, narrow window. When she peered in, Roberto was standing on the top of a bookshelf that rocked perilously. "Careful, buddy," she said, and then, "Oh no!"

Backing away as fast as she could, she flinched as the bookshelf hit the glass. A spiderweb of cracks spread across the window from the point of contact. She grabbed a log as thick as her arm from the ground and poked the glass right in the center of the web. It shattered and cascaded to the ground. Aside from a popping sound, it was surprisingly quiet. Only the immediate neighbors could have heard it and she was counting on everyone being at the festival.

Hoisting herself though the window was another matter, given her sprained ankle. But she wriggled and thrashed until she was inside, and then Roberto leapt right into her paws. She clutched him to her furry chest, and he rubbed his chin against her costume head.

Tears ran down her face inside, but there was nothing she could do about that.

"Where to, buddy?" she said, setting him down as gently as she could with big mitts.

He ran lightly across the gleaming hardwood and into the kitchen. Stopping in front of a door, he wove through her feet.

"Don't trip me, whatever you do," she said.

Opening the door, she flipped on the lights and crept downstairs.

CHAPTER TWENTY-SEVEN

I t only took three steps before she knew she'd found the right place. The smell penetrated the costume and almost made her gag.

"Oh no," she murmured, as she finished the descent. "How many?"

There were far more than she'd imagined. Cages literally stacked upon cages, many containing animals she'd never seen, nor imagined. It seemed unlikely she could get them all out in time, but she'd do what she could.

Glancing around, she saw no obvious way Roberto could have gotten in and out of the basement, but she wasn't about to explore every nook and cranny. There was a desk in the corner, above which she saw the plaque she'd seen on the cat-cam video. It had a foot-long gold fish affixed to it, and she didn't need to get close enough to know Zeke Mackey's name was engraved at the bottom. It had been hanging in his office on her first day—the day she'd also seen scratches and bruises on his legs, no doubt from his menagerie.

On a long shelf over the desk were a dozen taxidermy

animals—cats, dogs, a squirrel and even a possum. She wondered if he'd just happened upon them or had killed them himself. Either way, they seemed like creepy trophies.

Roberto stood against her leg and she felt his claws pierce the costume. They barely nicked her but it started her moving again. At last, she could fix this problem.

"Got it," she said. "We'll grab as many as we can right now." She hesitated, wondering if she should call Cori and Kinney, but decided against it. They had already done so much for her that she didn't want them caught in a scandal if it blew up. She had no doubt that the mayor's wrath was still swirling beneath his newly bland exterior. When he heard Zeke had betrayed him, the power of yoga might not contain it.

The next half hour passed in a blur. Up and down the stairs she went, leaving by the side door and filling Jon's van. She tried to keep her mind on the immediate task. If she thought about the snakes, lizards and even large spiders in the containers she carried, it would be her undoing. She moved carefully, knowing that a spilled spider was a busy spider.

"This must be what Cori meant by flooding," she said. "Well, this phobic is going to swim."

By the time she got to the bigger animals, she was drenched in sweat. Her thighs burned and her ankle sent off fireworks of pain. There was no way she could carry the larger crates upstairs and outside and they wouldn't all fit in the van. But she had planned ahead: Nick's hockey bag was filled with burlap sacks that had covered his shrubbery through the winter.

Opening the first door, she reached in with her big costume glove and grabbed a wild-eyed creature by the scruff. She placed it in a sack, twisted it closed with a plastic tie and moved on to the next. Some animals squealed in terror as she freed them, others leapt right into the bag. A few clung to the bars so hard she had to poke them out with a meat hook she found leaning in the corner.

Soon, there were just two full crates left in a dark corner near the furnace. She could tell by the familiar chirruping that the bigger pen held Letitia's long-lost family. Rounding them up was going to be a formidable task, so she deferred it by carrying the bagged animals upstairs as gently as possible.

Downstairs she went, hopefully for the last time. Bending over one of the crates, she gasped. It held a young wolf with eerie amber eyes. It crouched in the corner, growling, and she knew she couldn't risk handling it with only the bunny costume for protection. As much as it grieved her, she'd have to leave this one for experts.

The capybaras she couldn't abandon, but it was going to be challenging. The mama was more than a hundred pounds and there was simply no way to get her into a sack, let alone carry her upstairs. She would have to carry the babies and pray that mama would follow like a dog and willingly hop into the van after them. It was her only idea, and it had to work.

"What do you think?" she asked Roberto.

He rubbed against her leg, mewing urgently. The cat had never looked so agitated as he did in this moment.

"I hear you, buddy. This is not my idea of a good time, either." She leaned over, unlatched the pen and grabbed one of the capybara pups. "Here, piggy piggy piggy," she called to mama.

The big capybara, with its long square nose, came running and the impact knocked her backwards so hard sparks shot through her head and everything went black.

WHEN SHE OPENED HER EYES, she was sitting slouched against the wall, with the rabbit head lying beside her on the floor. Roberto was perched on her lap staring into the dark corner near the wolf cub.

"You going to live?" someone asked. "Stupid question. The answer is no."

"Hey, Zeke," she said, touching the back of her head and finding a large lump blooming. "I forgot to bring back your cat."

"It's okay," he said, moving forward. "I have yours now."

"He's coming with me," she said.

"But you're not going anywhere."

A shiver ran through her although she was pretty sure it was an idle threat. Zeke's movements were jerky and agitated, and when he came into the light, he was drenched in sweat.

"You can't keep me as part of your collection. My friends are on their way now."

"I doubt that," he said, smirking. "They were having a good time when I left." He paced around the small space and then picked up the meat hook she'd dropped on the floor. "You couldn't just leave me and my animals alone. It was none of your business. My exotics go to the best homes across the country, and even beyond."

"The ones that survive," she said. "The rest are buried on the Dayton estate."

"You lose some, you win some." After a pause, he added, "This isn't the ideal space for breeding, but I've expanded to a better facility."

His smirk faded, and his knuckles were white around the pole of the meat hook. As weird as it seemed, she sensed he valued these animals. Maybe not as pets, but as prized possessions. The fancy sports car they funded was just a bonus.

"Well, I can promise you that they'll be safe and happy somewhere else," she said.

"You're not in a position to make promises," he said, thumping the meat hook on the floor hard enough to make her jump. "And you're not taking my animals."

Roberto turned his head to the stairs and then kneaded her legs urgently.

"Check the driveway again," she said. "I think I've taken most of your animals already."

He turned and raced up the stairs. Minutes later more footsteps thumped on the stairs and Jon rushed into the room, followed by Remi and Mim.

Jon knelt beside her. "Are you okay?"

She nodded. "Did you get Zeke?"

"Nick's dealing with him now, and Sullivan, Carver and Tiller are dealing with Nick. Cori was trying to get a swing in."

"The animals?"

"Safe. Bridget's driving and Kinney is handling everything else discreetly."

He helped her to her feet and she asked, "How did you find me?"

"Nick and I saw the Easter bunny trip over the cherub and put two and two together. We spoke to Kinney and she knew how to find you." Annoyance vied with relief on his face. "She'd put a tracking device on my van."

Kinney came down the stairs. "No offense intended, Jon. But you never know what you need to know until you need to know it."

Evie's head swivelled. "Where's Roberto?"

"Outside, making sure everything is properly dealt with," Kinney said, grinning. "He almost tripped a police officer."

When they turned, however, Roberto was standing at the top of the stairs. He scraped at the carpet with one paw and offered a long meow.

"I couldn't agree more, buddy," Evie said. "This is just one big litter box."

CHAPTER TWENTY-EIGHT

E aster dinner had never tasted so good. Everyone gathered at Evie's after stopping at the only grocery store in town that was still open. Since Jon's van was too stinky for use after delivering the exotic animals to a temporary safe house, Tiller collected Nick's barbeque in his pickup. The men went out back to grill everything that could possibly be cooked over a fire. Meanwhile, the women made salads and told the story again and again from different points of view.

Evie sat at the kitchen table with Roberto in her lap, soaking it all in. Just weeks ago, she'd moved into this lonely, empty house. Now it was full, and her heart was even fuller.

"Welcome home, buddy," she whispered, scratching under the cat's chin. "You're the best thing that ever happened to me. And the worst. But mostly the best. I bet Clarence can shed some light on how you ended up in my door."

It seemed like it was all part of a greater mission that had hopefully played itself out. No more firings. No more freak accidents. No more broken hearts. Now she could put down roots and grow tall in the Dog Town sun. Surely she'd earned that.

"Bad news," Cori called from the front door. "There's a town car pulling into the driveway. Someone let the ass out of the ashram."

"You stole that line from Clarence," Evie called back. "But I'll give you a pass because you got him to come to the festival and buy me some time."

Setting Roberto on the floor, she got to her feet stiffly and reluctantly. The mayor would surely kill her happy buzz, but if she didn't go out, he'd come in.

"Wait," Remi said. Coming after her, she pressed Leo into Evie's arms. "You might need this."

"Maybe she'd rather have Thurston Howl," Arianna said, offering the fluffy red dog she'd brought along.

"Leo's more portable," Evie said, taking the beagle. Thurston was working his magic on her, but she wasn't ready to commit to anything serious yet.

The mayor waved and gestured to the passenger side, so she got in and settled the beagle in her lap. Cori jumped onto the hood of the car with her back to them.

"Must she?" Mayor Bradshaw said. "This is a City-owned vehicle."

"Cori rescued the wolf cub from Zeke's place single-handedly," Evie said. "I figure she can sit anywhere she wants today."

"Remind me to thank her," he said. "Where are these exotics beasts, anyway?"

"I'm not sure, actually. A safe house en route to a final home. According to Cori, the less I know the better."

"Fine, whatever." His tone was a trifle clipped, but his lips curved into a reluctant smile. "I actually came to offer you the role of chief of staff."

"That's... unexpected, sir." A month ago, it might have been a dream come true. Now it was tiring even to contemplate.

"And well earned," he said, smile turning beatific smile. "I suggest a week's retreat before you start. It will do your soul a world of good."

"My soul's in good order, but thank you. I won't be leaving my cat alone anytime soon."

The cat in question was now headbutting the windshield and the mayor tried shooing him. "Really, Evelyn. Can't you stop him?"

"He's unstoppable," she said. "That's how I discovered Zeke's secret collection."

The mayor shuddered. "I find the whole thing unbearably distasteful and I couldn't be more relieved it's been resolved quietly."

"What's happening with Zeke?"

"He won't be spared, I assure you. Thanks to you, however, the public will be. Now, let's talk about your promotion."

"We'll meet tomorrow, sir. As you can see, I have guests."

Most of the crowd had come out on the front porch. Nick was keeping an eye on the car, but when Jon came down the stairs to stand beside the passenger door, her brother felt free to give Hannah his full attention.

"The CCD will need to conduct a full sweep of your house before you start your new role," the mayor said. "If your cat is escaping, who knows what trouble will follow. After this, I can't afford to take any risks."

Evie leaned her head back, hugging Leo tight, and closed her eyes. She pulled a deep breath in through her nose and released through her mouth, just like the mayor advised. Then she did it again. And again. Her heart rate seemed to slow and Leo started snoring gently.

"Evelyn," the mayor said. "Are you asleep?"

Keeping her eyes closed, she said, "Just connecting with my heart chakra, sir. To see if your offer works for me."

"Excuse me? This is the job of a lifetime."

He sounded decidedly more alert, and she opened her eyes.

"Someone's lifetime," she said. "I love the idea of doing good work for Dog Town, but I think my days as political staff are over."

"Evelyn, I insist. There's simply no one else I can trust."

"I want a quiet life, sir. You, more than anyone, can understand that." She pressed her open palm to the glass of the passenger window, and Jon did the same from the other side.

"How sweet," Mayor Bradshaw said. "But I'll thank you not to leave prints on the glass."

"I'll help you recruit a new chief, sir. Then you can back my service dog project. A year from now you'll be making headlines for offering the very best therapy dogs on the planet. Another claim to fame for Dog Town."

He pursed his lips. "I'm not sold on this whole therapy dog schtick. If everyone did their inner work, there would be no need for therapy dogs."

"I got threatened with a meat hook today, sir. Hugging this therapy dog is doing wonders right now."

Leo's head lolled back and he stared at the mayor upside down.

Shaking his head, the mayor said, "Bring me your proposal."

"I will. Thank you."

She reached for the latch and he held up his hand.

"There's a small issue percolating. We may need to have a chat with your resourceful friends." He gestured to his human hood ornament. "I've had a few calls today. Nothing to be alarmed about."

"What happened?"

"Some puppies have gone missing." He checked his phone. "Leann Cosgrove lost a beagle and Ruth Banks a Maltese." He scrolled down. "In all, about a dozen breeders have lost a single purebred pup."

"Mayor, that's terrible! It sounds like an organized hit."

"Now, now, you worry too much. But your little squad might be able to offer some advice."

"I'm sure they'll help us."

His smile blazed, almost back to full force. "Excellent. I knew you'd step up, given the chance. I always believed in you, Evelyn."

"I'm not taking the chief's job, sir, I'm sorry."

"But—"

She gathered Leo in her arms. "You're just going to have to be at peace with what is, whatever that is."

"I never appreciated your humor, Evelyn." He reached for his door latch, too. "If I may, I'll just pop in for a moment and—"

"Not tonight, sir, I'm sorry. But I'll bring you some left-overs tomorrow."

Jon dropped an arm around her shoulders as she got out of the car. "Everything okay?"

"Yes, no and maybe," she said.

The mayor put the car in reverse. Cori hopped off the hood of the car, treating him to a double flipping wave.

"Remind me about my future?" she asked Evie as the town car drove off.

"Cori Hogan for mayor," Evie said. "In the meantime, the chief of staff role is wide open if you're interested."

With a scornful laugh, Cori ran up the stairs and joined the crowd as it moved back inside. Evie followed slowly, with Jon on one side, and Gilda on the other. Roberto did a brisk, tight figure eight and almost tripped her again.

"That's the problem with Dog Town," she told Jon, side-stepping the cat. "You barely get over one problem and the next is waiting to trip you up."

Jon gave her a hug before going inside. "True enough. All we can do is savor each moment."

The door closed behind them and the crowd of people, dogs and one very happy cat swallowed them up in a warm embrace. Despite some treacherous early twists, Evie's ninth life seemed to be turning out just fine.

Are you curious about the mysterious missing puppies, and whether or not Hannah Pemberton finds true love when she moves back home to Dorset Hills? If so, get *Great and Small in Dog Town*.

Please sign up for my author newsletter at **Sandyrideout.com** to receive the FREE prequel, *Ready or Not in Dog Town*, as well as *A Dog with Two Tales*, the prequel to the Bought-the-Farm series. You'll also get the latest news and far too many pet photos.

Before you move on to the next book, if you would be so kind as to leave a review of this one, that would be great. I appreciate the feedback and support. Reviews stoke the fires of my creativity!

Other Books by Sandy Rideout and Ellen Riggs

Dog Town Series:

- *Ready or Not in Dog Town* (The Beginning)
- *Bitter and Sweet in Dog Town* (Labor Day)
- *A Match Made in Dog Town* (Thanksgiving)
- *Lost and Found in Dog Town* (Christmas)
- *Calm and Bright in Dog Town* (Christmas)
- *Tried and True in Dog Town* (New Year's)
- *Yours and Mine in Dog Town* (Valentine's Day)
- *Nine Lives in Dog Town* (Easter)
- *Great and Small in Dog Town* (Memorial Day)
- *Bold and Blue in Dog Town* (Independence Day)
- *Better or Worse in Dog Town* (Labor Day)

Boxed Sets:

- *Mischief in Dog Town - Books 1-3*
- *Mischief in Dog Town - Books 4-7*
- *Mischief in Dog Town - Books 8-10*

Bought-the-Farm Cozy Mystery Series

- *A Dog with Two Tales (prequel)*
- *Dogcatcher in the Rye*
- *Dark Side of the Moo*
- *A Streak of Bad Cluck*
- *Till the Cat Lady Sings*
- *Alpaca Lies*
- *Twas the Bite Before Christmas*
- *Swine and Punishment*
- *Don't Rock the Goat*
- *Swan with the Wind*

Made in the USA
Las Vegas, NV
08 October 2022

56752198R00136